Sissi Flegel

# Forbidden to Love

Aus dem Deutschen
von Sally-Ann Spencer



Thienemann

# Isa

English was a **dead loss** that Thursday.

Isa had brought along the new issue of *Bravo Girl.* She wanted to show it to her friend Nadja without the others seeing, but Nadja came, saw and **squealed**. In no time the others were crowding around her desk.

"What's up? Let's have a look! Show us what you're looking at!"

Yvonne grabbed a corner of the magazine, pulled and then squealed just like Nadja. "That's you!" she shouted at the top of her voice.

The cat was out of the bag.

"How did you manage that?"

"Does that mean you've been **discovered**?"

"Where did you get all the gear?"

"Who did your make-up?"

"My God, *Bravo Girl*! You don't still read that, do you? You're way too old! How come you're in it?"

"Got any more questions?" asked Isa, half joking, half horrified.

"Well, go on, tell us! We want to hear everything. Those photos are something else, huh?" said Nadja.

The others thought so too.

"It was luck," said Isa. "A girl from my riding club

---

dead loss – totaler Reinfall; to squeal – kreischen;
to discover – entdecken

knows someone who works for *Bravo Girl*, and she agreed to model for them. But when the **crew** showed up with the clothes for the shoot, none of the sweaters, trousers or anything fitted her. But *I* happened to be the right size, and so …"

"… they did the shoot with you instead. Wow, how cool is that!" said Nadja excitedly, but with a tinge of **envy**.

"How on earth did they get your hair so straight?"

Isa was always **struggling with** her hair. It wasn't straight, but it wasn't wavy or curly either. It was **wiry** – and almost impossible to control.

She'd tried just about everything – cutting it short and growing it long – but it never ended up the way she wanted it. Right now she was growing it again, but a lot of the time it just stuck out from her head at a right angle.

"My hair looks amazing," said Isa enthusiastically. "They soaked it and then tugged so hard while they were drying it that I thought my **scalp** would come off. It never works that well when I **blow-dry** it at home …"

"It looks really great, but it doesn't look like you," concluded Nadja critically.

"And did they ask you loads of questions about school, your family, your hobbies and all that?" Julia wanted to know.

"Yeah, but I wasn't going to **fall for** that, and so I

---

crew – Kamerateam; envy – Neid;
to struggle with sth – sich mit etw. herumquälen;
wiry – drahtig; scalp – Kopfhaut; to blow-dry – fönen;
to fall for sth – auf etw. hereinfallen

told them a heap of old rubbish. I mean, it's not really anyone's business whether I'm any good at maths, English or biology, is it? And if I **can't stand** my brother, that's my problem too."

The others nodded in agreement. "But the stuff you said about riding, you meant that, didn't you?" probed Julia. "And you told them that you're **editor** of the school magazine."

Isa nodded. "Interviews are totally tricky. You don't want to be a complete flop – you know, look utterly desperate or something. But you don't want to give too much away either. So what do you do? You have to duck and dive. The stuff I said about riding is true, but the other stuff about school and my family is only sort of true – although it's not a massive lie either." Isa shrugged. "Whichever way, you feel like a **fraud** at the end of it."

"I bet," said Nadja, drumming her fingers up and down on the page. "But it's dead cool all the same. Are your parents all right about it?"

Isa shrugged again. "No idea. I haven't told them yet."

Isa was feeling bad about that. In her family there was only one strict rule: secrets were banned. That was because her parents wanted to treat themselves and their children, Isa and Paul, with respect and as equals. And that, they explained, was only possible when you trusted each other. As far as they were concerned, keeping secrets was **petty** and degrading. And

---

to not be able to stand sth – etw. nicht ertragen können;
editor – Redakteur; fraud – Betrüger;
petty – belanglos

in any case, secrets always come out in the end, and then what? The trust is gone or at any rate permanently dented. Isa and her brother had realized early on that it wasn't worth the risk, and they'd always stuck to the rule.

Isa ruffled her hair. She hadn't had time to tell her parents when she'd first been asked about the interview and photos for *Bravo Girl.*

She could have told them later, of course, but what if they'd said no? And anyway, there was always the chance that the piece wouldn't be printed, and then it would be pointless to ask and risk a conflict. That would only upset everyone too – or so she'd told herself. So she'd decided to keep quiet for a bit. And now look where that had got her! A **guilty conscience** and the nasty job of **owning up to** the photos as well as to having been less than honest. Great. That spoils it all, she thought, and pulled a face. If only things hadn't happened so suddenly, and if only she'd stopped to think … But it was too late now to change anything. The only option was absolute honesty. She decided to **take the bull by the horns**.

At lunchtime she went home and positioned the magazine on the dining-room table. "Mum," she **yelled**, "can you come here a minute? There's something I have to show you. It's really important!"

"Can't it wait?" pleaded Isa's mum. "I've had a really stressful morning."

---

guilty conscience – schlechtes Gewissen; to own up to sth – etw. beichten; to take the bull by the horns – den Stier bei den Hörnern packen; to yell – rufen/schreien

"Why? What's up?" asked Isa, grateful for the **reprieve**.

Her mum plodded barefoot out of the kitchen to explain. That morning she hadn't had time to make lunch because she'd been called to the rescue of her sister, Florentine, who'd phoned her in despair. So she'd bought lunch in town instead: cutlet in bread crumbs (cold) and potato salad (freezing). Not the kind of lunch anyone could get excited about, least of all Isa's mum.

"You could have got pizza instead," grumbled Isa's younger brother Paul. "Or something from **Maccy Ds**. Right, Isa?"

Isa nodded and fished out a large chunk of onion from the cold, slithery salad. She dumped it on the edge of her plate. "So why did Florentine need **rescuing**? And what from?"

"I bet it's got something to do with her boyfriend. Has he crashed his car or something? That would be a disaster! I'm still waiting for him to pick me up from school in it, like he promised. You know, a taxi service like that would be great for my image ..." Paul carried on **chewing**. "So what's the story? Is the car OK?"

His mum nodded. "The car's OK. But everything else looks fairly grim. Florentine's having trouble with Bert-Wolfram."

Paul shrugged, pushed his plate to one side and stood up. "Mouldy old relationships just aren't my thing. I'll be in my room, all right?"

---

reprieve – Begnadigung; Maccy Ds – McDonald's;
to rescue – retten; to chew – kauen

"So why did she call you?" Isa demanded. "Florentine's usually perfectly **capable** of sorting things out by herself."

Isa liked her aunt. She was her mum's younger sister and she'd only just turned thirty. She was fun to be around, full of energy, always ready for new adventures, attractive and totally cool. Isa wanted to look as good as her, dress just like her – usually in black – and be every bit as successful and strong as her. Except she didn't want to be an **interior designer**; she wanted to be a journalist.

"This time it looks serious," said Isa's mum. "She's had a funny feeling for a while. Things haven't been like they were before. And this morning she found out for certain that he's got another girlfriend. Which is bad enough, of course, but there's worse. She'd tried asking him loads of times, but he always denied it, the **coward**. And that's what Florentine can't understand – she says that if the situation changes, it's only fair to be honest."

Isa nodded and thought of the photos in *Bravo Girl*. "But sometimes you don't get around to it right away. And then you forget about it, and by the time you remember, things have changed and you still can't **come clean**."

"Well, that's sometimes true, but in this case Florentine's boyfriend had plenty of time and opportunity to come up with a straight answer to her questions. 'Treat others the way you'd like them to treat you', that's my motto."

---

capable – fähig; interior designer – Innenarchitekt;
coward – Feigling; to come clean – reinen Tisch machen

Isa had always liked Florentine's boyfriend. He never asked any of the usual **tedious** questions that other adults ask. How's school? Do you like your teachers? What about your **grades**? What's your favourite subject? Whenever he and Florentine visited them, he always asked her about her latest feature for the school magazine or about sport, but that was it ... Sport – oh God! Isa looked at the time.

"Mum, I have to go! Astra and Felix will be waiting for me. If I don't hurry, I'll be seriously late!"

A few minutes later she had wheeled her bike out of the garage and was racing down the street.

The **paddock** was a fair distance from the house – she needed at least fifteen minutes to get there, but she'd never been late, and with a bit of luck she'd make it this time too.

She did.

The riding **stables** were made up of the Langer family's house, the stable itself and two new smaller buildings for the horses' food, equipment and all the stuff you need for running a riding school. For five years now, Isa had been going riding three times a week, and the time she spent at the stables was an important part of her life. Of course, her seventeen-year-old boyfriend, Felix, also had something to do with it.

He was waiting for her already, and as always he relieved her of her bike and **propped** it **up against** the wall.

---

tedious – langweilig; grade – Schulnote; paddock – Koppel; stable – Stall; to prop sth up against sth – etw. gegen etw. lehnen

Isa had taken Paul to the stables with her once, but when he saw how Felix Langer treated his sister, he stared wide-eyed and open-mouthed. "Isa can do that herself," he said, once he'd finally pulled himself together. "Why are you doing it for her?"

Felix went a bit red, but then answered coolly: "That's the way it should be. Don't you know that?"

That was **the last straw** for Paul. From then on riding and everything that went with it was totally out as far as he was concerned.

Isa found Felix's behaviour old-fashioned and a bit exaggerated too, but that didn't stop her slamming on the brakes, leaping off her bike and pushing it in his direction every time she got to the stables.

"How's it going?" asked Isa, and gave Felix a kiss. "What's Astra been up to?"

Astra was "her" horse. She was **capricious**, moody and pig-headed, and Isa always had to show her who was boss. But Isa liked that – a **dull** horse wouldn't be half as much fun.

"Everything's fine," Felix assured her, putting his arm around her shoulders.

They walked over to the stable together. Astra raised her head, looked towards them and **whinnied**.

"She's in a good mood today," said Isa, leading Astra out into the open. Felix followed her with Joringel. They tethered the horses and started **grooming**.

Isa pulled a few horsehairs out of the brush. "I've got a bit of a problem," she said.

---

to be the last straw – das Fass zum Überlaufen bringen; capricious – launisch; dull – langweilig; to whinny – wiehern; to groom – striegeln

"Yeah? Bad grades or something?" asked Felix. "It can't be too bad, or else you wouldn't look so happy."

Isa laughed. "Just because you can't see my worries doesn't mean they're not there."

Felix put the brush down and gave Isa a hug. "Well, fire away; maybe I can help."

Isa snuggled up to him for a moment and then pulled away. She took the magazine out of her rucksack, turned to the critical page and pushed it under Felix's nose.

He glanced at the cover. "I thought you would choose your reading matter more carefully," he said. "As a **budding journalist** you should at least …" Then he gave a low whistle. "I see, look at that, I only just noticed – that's you!" He studied the text with great concentration, looked at the photos, closed the magazine and laid it down on Isa's rucksack.

"The photos are good and the profile is really positive," he said at last. "But what I'd like to know is: how did you of all people end up in *Bravo Girl*."

Isa filled him in and **summed up**: "So you see, there wasn't anything I could do about it. I didn't take the whole thing seriously at the time, so I didn't tell my parents. And now things are really awkward …"

Felix nodded. "I can see that. But you'll just have to deal with it. Ducking the issue won't help, nor will hiding it or trying to **gloss over** it." He leant his head to one side and smiled at her. "One of the things I really like about you, Isa, is how **brave** you are."

---

budding journalist – begabter Nachwuchsjournalist;
to sum up – zusammenfassen;
to gloss over – unter den Teppich kehren; brave – mutig

Isa looked at him. Felix was always well dressed. He never wore loud clothes and he didn't try to **jazz himself up** with wacky haircuts; but it would never have occurred to anyone to think of him as boring. She sighed. "OK, I'll be brave," she said resolutely.

"Good on you. But there's no need to go peddling those photos around, you know!"

"Felix!" exclaimed Isa in horror. "What do you take me for?"

He laughed. "Well, hurry up then. I thought we were going riding today – or maybe our supermodel doesn't feel like it?"

Isa would have liked to throw the brush at him. Instead she stuck out her tongue. "You shouldn't **mock the afflicted**," she said. "That's really mean, you know."

It took a good thirty minutes for them to finish grooming. Then they saddled the horses and rode slowly out of the yard. The sun was shining brightly.

---

to jazz oneself up – sich aufpeppen;
Don't mock the afflicted. – Wer den Schaden hat, braucht für den Spott nicht zu sorgen.

# Florentine's Dishonourable Lover

The house was deathly quiet.

Isa had a quick shower, pulled on the long, black skirt that Florentine had once given her, searched for her T-shirt with the garish orange and pink swirls, rummaged through her wardrobe and all her drawers, couldn't find it, finally located it in the tumble-dryer, pulled it over her head and **jangled** the little silver ring in her belly button. Rather than revising maths, which in view of the **impending** exam would have been more useful, she picked out two little bottles from her **nail-varnish** collection and sat down at her desk. With great concentration she painted her fingernails half orange, half pink, in diagonal sections. The colours exactly matched her mood, thought Isa, pleased. She liked trying out new looks.

She heard her mum come in with Paul. "She has to be in here somewhere," Paul shouted at the top of his voice. "I can see her riding-hat!"

The door was **yanked** open and Paul rushed in.

Isa shook her hands to dry her nails. "Watch out," she yelled at her brother, "don't touch!"

"Why didn't you tell us?" He slammed a copy of *Bravo Girl* onto the table.

---

to jangle sth – mit etw. klimpern; impending – bevorstehend; nail-varnish – Nagellack; to yank – reißen

"Yes, why all the secrecy all of a sudden?" her mum demanded. "I thought we said no secrets, hmm?"

"I know," said Isa **meekly**. "I was going to tell you straight after school, but your rescue mission to Florentine was more important than the fate of your own daughter." Isa looked at her mum **reproachfully**.

The telephone rang.

Paul darted off and picked up the receiver. "Isa, it's for you," he yelled. "It's Nadja's brother, the one with the big ears."

Isa snatched the phone away from him. "Sorry about that," she said breathlessly. "My brother's awful. He's got nothing to do with me."

"Hey Isa, my sister's just shown me *Bravo Girl*. You look amazing – dead cool. Congratulations!"

Isa laughed, feeling **flattered**.

"I don't look that good!" she said. "No need to get carried away. The whole thing was an **accident** really, that's all, honestly."

"We're going to the pub later – want to come? Everyone'll be there, and I bet they've seen the photos. How about it?"

Isa agreed to go along. She'd already forgotten about the maths exam.

Her mum leafed through the magazine and shook her head a few times. When Isa had finished on the phone, she pulled her down next to her on the sofa.

"So how did you end up in the magazine? And why did you keep it so quiet? I just don't get it – you'd never be able to hide something like that!"

---

meekly – kleinlaut; reproachfully – vorwurfsvoll;
flattered – geschmeichelt; accident – Zufall

Once again Isa summed up what had happened and finished off by saying: “I wasn’t supposed to be in it, honest. If I hadn’t happened to be there and if the clothes hadn’t happened to fit me, no one would have been interested in me at all. I just **got dragged into** the whole thing and then it was too late to back out again. It all happened so quickly, Mum, honest. You’ve got to understand.”

“I do understand, but it still doesn’t explain why you didn’t tell us about it straight away …”

The doorbell rang. It was Florentine. She rushed through the door, chucked her bag into a corner, slammed her car keys onto the table in the hall and threw herself into an armchair.

“I can’t stand it,” she said wildly. “I just can’t stand it. I won’t **put up with** this wretchedness any longer. He’s driving me absolutely mad! This stupid, disturbed, neurotic **jerk** – I’m going to get rid of him for once and for all!”

“You do that,” said Isa’s mum. “But first of all come through to the kitchen and have a nice cup of tea.”

“What’s wrong?” asked Paul nosily. “Is your boyfriend getting on your nerves? The one with the stupid name, Bert-Wolfram.”

Florentine shook her head vigorously. “Oh, he’s been getting on my nerves all right, but that’s all over now. The **schmuck**! All over! I’m finished with him. Forever! How can anyone be so blind, so stupid, so dumb!”

---

to get dragged into sth – in etw. reingezogen werden; to put up with sth – etw. aushalten; jerk – Trottel; schmuck – Blödmann

"Hang on, who's stupid, blind and dumb? You or Bert-Wolfram?" asked Isa.

"Me, of course!" said Florentine, blowing her nose. "You live in the same flat together, work together, share the same friends and God knows what else, and then all of a sudden it happens. It's the kind of situation you've only ever read about in **gossip mags** at the hairdresser's: a blonde ..."

"Does she drive a Manta?" asked Paul, his ears pricking up.

"Err no. Why do you ask?"

"Because she's blonde," explained Paul impatiently. "Why did the blonde climb the glass wall?"

"To see what was on the other side," answered Florentine without thinking. She ran her fingers through her jet-black hair. "But I'm not really in the mood for jokes, not after listening to Bert-Wolfram tell me that he doesn't know what all the **fuss** is about. According to him, the whole thing was just a short-lived **fling** and has absolutely nothing, zero, to do with our relationship. What century is this man living in? Has he even heard of women's **lib**?"

"He's a nasty old macho," decided Paul. "Women are just sexual objects for him."

"Paul!" exclaimed his mum in alarm. "Where did you get that from?"

"From dad, of course."

"I'll be having words with him," said his mum. "Just wait until he gets home!"

---

gossip magazine – Klatschzeitschrift; fuss – Aufregung; fling – Affäre; lib – Befreiung

"Well, maybe he didn't really mean it," suggested Isa.

"Who? Dad?"

"No, Bert-Wolfram. I mean, maybe he just saw her a few times, had a chat, went for a coffee ..."

Florentine **howled**. "For coffee! Don't make me laugh! He was living a double life, the worm, and was hoping that I'd never find out."

"So what happens now? You've found out, but what are you going to do?" asked Isa.

"I'm ..." Florentine gave a sob and blew her nose vigorously. "After I found out and he kept denying it, there were only two options: no end of horror or a horrible end." Florentine started to cry.

Paul looked at her pityingly, and then stuck the copy of *Bravo Girl* under her nose. "Take a look at this – Isa's in it."

Florentine cast a tearful eye over the brightly coloured pictures and then squealed. "My God, that's Isa! Just look at her! Isa, you look great – congratulations!"

"Isa just got lucky," said Isa's mum, trying to play it down. "Don't make her head any bigger, OK? The tea's ready. Don't you two have homework to be getting on with?"

Paul nodded. "Isa, they want to talk woman-to-woman, and we kids aren't needed." He plunged his hand into the biscuit-tin. Before he reached the door, he turned back to face Florentine: "I think it's good that you're rid of your macho boyfriend and can start looking for another partner, but I must say, your tim-

---

to howl – aufjaulen

ing's terrible. Couldn't you have waited until he'd picked me up from school in his **flashy** car?"

"In the heat of the moment it must have **slipped my mind**," said Florentine. "Maybe when you're older you'll understand."

"I already understand," said Paul. "Some things just can't be delayed."

"That's exactly it," said Florentine, and burst into tears.

Isa felt like hugging her aunt, but Paul was tugging on her sleeve and dragging her away. "I'm off now," she said as she got to the door. "Johannes and the others are waiting for me."

"When will you be back?" asked her mum, pouring Florentine a cup of tea. "Nine-ish or so? Don't forget you've got school tomorrow. Have you done your homework?"

"It's all taken care of," said Isa quickly. "No worries."

And with that she was gone.

Isa **flunked** maths and English was a disaster too. She only had to think of physics and chemistry and she started to feel ill. Things weren't looking good for her at school. There were only two options: **revise** around the clock or do absolutely nothing. And there were so many gaps in her knowledge she might as well give up. Isa decided on the second option. She went out with her friends, met Felix at the stables, went rid-

---

flashy – protzig; to slip sb's mind – etw. vergessen;
to flunk – in einer Prüfung durchfallen;
to revise – auf eine Prüfung lernen

ing as often as she could and tried to **avoid** her parents. She also started a two-page article on the topic "Daily Life at the Stables – Everything You Need to Know about Horses and Riding". There were a couple of books she'd have to read to back up her **evidence**.

But her parents were getting more and more concerned about her future at school. Because of their policy on honesty, they knew all about her botched exams.

When Isa announced that she would be spending three evenings a week at a self-defence course for women as part of the research for her next-but-one article, her parents' tolerance finally snapped. The time had come to lay down the law.

"But what if I write a rubbish article? Is that what you want? And anyway – if I'm learning self-defence, I won't be wasting my time. In fact, if you think about it properly, I'd be **killing two birds with one stone**. I mean, you don't want me to be assaulted, do you?"

"Don't be ridiculous," snapped her dad. "No one would wish that on you, least of all your parents. But we don't like the idea of you re-sitting your exams next year either. So, how do we **handle** this?"

Isa wrinkled her nose. "Well, I can't give up riding, and I can't stop seeing Felix or my friends. Everyone needs friends, you know. If you don't have friends, you can't do anything at all. Even you must see that.

---

to avoid – meiden; evidence – Ergebnis; to kill two birds with one stone – zwei Fliegen mit einer Klappe schlagen;
to handle sth – etw. handhaben

Besides, I've still got the magazine to look after … How on earth am I supposed to manage all that?"

"That's just it," said her mum. "You do too much in your free time and not enough for school. Now if you were a **genius**, things would be different …"

"You see," Isa interjected, "if you'd given me the right genes in the first place, we wouldn't be having this argument. Fundamentally, it's all your fault. I can't help it if I'm not clever enough."

"But you can help being lazy, and it's time you realized that. The holidays start in a fortnight, right?" Her dad leafed through the calendar. "You've got two weeks of holiday. And in these two weeks you're going to sit down and revise. No doubt, I'll be able to find someone to help you."

"You can't do that to me!" yelled Isa. "I can revise on my own. And in the holidays I want to be on holiday. School's very stressful, you know, and everyone needs a **break** sometime. Holidays are there for a reason …"

"Yes – to go back over what you've learnt, to fill in the gaps and to catch up on anything you missed during term." Isa's dad wouldn't let her finish. "Without **extra tuition** you'll end up repeating the year. And that would be far worse than just revising in the holidays. I'll get hold of someone right away."

"Well I guess I don't have a choice then," said Isa reluctantly. She thought for a moment, then brightened up: "Maybe you could find a nice young student?"

---

genius – Genie; break – Pause;
extra tuition – Nachhilfeunterricht

She smiled at her dad and gave him an affectionate pat. She twisted her belly button ring with her other hand.

"He'll be the **oldest**, ugliest **fogey** I can find," her dad said bluntly. "Someone who's more interested in the gaps in your knowledge than the ring through your navel."

"I can't wait to meet him," said Isa. Then she suddenly thought of something. "Does that mean you'll be going on holiday without me? Can I still come to Tuscany too?"

"You'll be staying here to revise," decided her father. Something in his tone warned Isa not to argue.

**Fed up** and frustrated she retreated to her room.

But things turned out very differently. And all because of Florentine.

She'd been serious about getting rid of her boyfriend. She ordered a **removal van** to take away his stuff. She shoved a bit of paper into the driver's hand – it was the address of an architects' office, owned by the love-rat himself.

Then she drove over to see her sister, Isa's mother. Kicking out Bert-Wolfram had made her feel a hundred years younger, she announced. And that called for a celebration – she was inviting the whole family for a meal at the best Italian restaurant.

"But wasn't that one of your old **haunts**?" asked Isa's mum. "Won't it bring back old memories? Are you sure you can cope?"

---

old fogey – alter Kauz; to be fed up – die Nase voll haben; removal van – Möbelwagen; haunt – Stammlokal

“No problem. I’m completely over him,” declared Florentine. “Well, at any rate, I hope so.”

But while they were sitting there, toasting Florentine’s future happiness with red wine and apple juice, a man came up to their table. It was him – the stupid, disturbed, neurotic jerk – the schmuck.

With a theatrical gesture he announced, “My leaving present,” and let a plain brown envelope **waft** onto the table as he walked quickly away.

The candle flickered and the little vase with its lone red **carnation** gave a wobble.

Florentine grabbed hold of the envelope. “What the hell was that about? What’s he up to now?” She ripped open the envelope. “Oh God!” she shouted. “You’re never going to believe this.” She looked at the others, then slammed two plane tickets onto the table. “What I am supposed to do with these?”

“What are they?” asked Paul eagerly. “Come on, **spill the beans**; you know we don’t keep secrets.”

“This isn’t a secret; this is a problem,” said Florentine helplessly. She was trying not to sob. “It’s like this: we were planning a holiday together. A package holiday on an island for a week: sport, sea, sun and sand … The idea came to us on New Year’s Eve, after Bert-Wolfram had heard his secretary going on about some pretty little island in the Aegean. Anyway, the first thing we did in January was to go to a travel agent’s and book the flight and hotel. I’d forgotten all about it. After the shock and anger of what happened, I guess it didn’t seem important.”

---

to waft – schweben; carnation – Nelke;
Spill the beans! – Sag schon!

"So what are you going to do?" asked Paul in a **matter-of-fact** tone. "Go on your own?"

"Of course not!" said Florentine firmly.

"Have a look to see if you've paid," suggested Isa's dad.

Florentine **leafed through** the documents, read the small print on one page and announced with fury: "He paid the balance yesterday. What a worm! He wants me to feel bad about it."

"I expect he was trying to do the right thing," said Isa.

Florentine snorted.

The waiter set down a platter of antipasti in the middle of the table.

Paul **impaled** a piece of baby octopus on his fork, stared in fascination at the pale lilac-coloured suckers, and said casually: "I'd offer to go with you, really, I would, but I'm already set to go camping with a few **mates** from school."

"Thanks for offering," said Florentine. "Why don't you two use the tickets? It's all been paid for: flight, hotel, everything. Why don't you take them?" She thrust the envelope towards her sister.

Isa's mum shook her head. "We're off to Tuscany, remember?"

"Of course." Florentine shoved the envelope under her plate. "I'd forgotten about that."

"You should go by yourself," urged Isa. "I bet there are loads of men out there. You'll be able to find a new one, no problem."

---

matter-of-fact – sachlich; to leaf through – durchblättern; to impale – aufspießen; mate – Kumpel

"Men!" Florentine blew her nose. "I never want to have anything to do with them again."

"OK, calm down," said Isa. "At least the other half of humanity is made up of women, like us."

Florentine looked at her **niece**. "Why don't you go? With a friend?"

"Isa will be busy revising," her dad cut in. His voice was firm. "She won't have time."

"But she could revise for the first week and go on holiday for the second. That would be OK, wouldn't it?" asked Florentine.

"There's no need to **reward** her for her laziness." Isa's dad shook his head in disapproval.

"So how about a week in a beach club?" Florentine asked her niece. "It's on an island somewhere in the Med, just off the Turkish coast."

"Does it have horses?" Isa **dunked** a piece of bread into the puddle of olive oil on her plate.

Florentine shook her head. "I think you can only do watersports and aerobics."

"Not my thing," said Isa determinedly. "And anyway, I've got to revise."

Florentine nodded. "I'll phone around a bit tomorrow. Maybe someone will fancy it ... Typical of that idiot to **drop** me **in it**, even after we've **split up**."

Everyone laughed.

The waiter arrived with the main course and refilled their glasses. "Enjoy your meal." In no time he was back again with a package.

"A young man left this at the door. It's for some-

---

niece – Nichte; to reward – belohnen; to dunk – eintunken; to drop sb in it – jmd. reinlegen; to split up – sich trennen one called Florentine. He said she would be sitting at this table …"

Florentine groaned. She seized the package, tore open the brown paper, ripped through a layer of tissue paper, and stared **in disbelief**: it was a miniscule black bikini featuring three well-placed stars made of gold.

Isa picked up the white card and read: "Good luck with it!" She raised her head. "There's no two ways about it: that man is a total **slime-ball.**"

Florentine nodded. "Isa, love, take a piece of advice from my **trove** of experience. You can't love a schmuck. If a man isn't lovable, there's nothing to love about him. Got it? So be careful who you fall for. I'm your aunt after all; it's my duty to make sure you're happy!"

---

in disbelief – ungläubig; slime-ball – Ekel; trove – Schatz

# A Heady Mix

True to his word, Isa's dad didn't **waste** a single second in **tracking down** a retired teacher with sufficient energy and determination to guide Isa back through the basics in all the main subjects. Since her case was critical and he had plenty of time on his hands, he agreed to start tutoring the very next day.

Isa was furious. "Couldn't it have waited? I need at least a few days to mentally prepare."

Her dad just growled and gave her a hostile look.

They didn't hear anything from Florentine for a while.

Then one evening, about a week later, she **dropped by**. "I can't get rid of those tickets," she said. "But I've tried on the bikini and it fits perfectly. It looks far too good not to wear it!"

"So you're going?" probed her sister.

Florentine nodded. "But it won't be much fun by myself ... Are you sure Isa can't come? I mean, surely she's earned a few days off, now that she's kept **her nose to the grindstone**."

She talked on and on and on until Isa's parents ran

---

to waste – verschwenden; to track down – ausfindig machen; drop by – vorbeischauen; to keep one's nose to the grindstone – sich bei der Arbeit ranhalten

out of arguments. They **reluctantly** gave their permission: Isa could spend a week with her aunt on the island. Isa was already in bed when her aunt burst in to tell her the news.

"I thought I told you I didn't want to go!" she protested. "I'm supposed to be home alone in the holidays, and I've already got stuff planned. I've invited thousands of people to a party, and I can't just uninvite them. Florentine, you've got to see it my way!"

But Florentine refused to **be put off**. "Of course, you can uninvite them. You can throw a party some time later – you can have it in my flat, and I'll even help you set it up. How about it? That way you'll kill two birds with one stone. And in the resort you'll be able to do as much sport as you like – it won't be boring, I promise. You'll get to meet new people and have all kinds of new experiences ... Just think what a great **topic** for an article that will make! You won't get another chance like this, Isa! We'll eat together, but apart from that you can do what you want."

In the end Isa gave in – it was the thought of the article and a week without revision that **clinched** it.

The next few days were frantic: school, the **crammer course**, riding, shopping ... Isa was determined to buy a little round **felt** hat with a brim, in order to stand out from the other tourists. And some notepads and pencils, of course. She wanted to be able to **jot down** her

---

reluctantly – widerwillig; to be put off – sich beirren lassen;
topic – Thema; to clinch sth – etw. entscheiden;
crammer course – „Pauk"-Kurs; felt – Filz;
to jot down – notieren

observations, experiences and impressions while they were fresh in her mind. She could already see herself, reclining in a deckchair on the beach, watching other people and scribbling down her incisive comments, smiling to herself …

Inga, one of Florentine's friends, had **volunteered** to drive them to the airport. The day before Whit Sunday, they were ready to go. Inga beeped her horn outside, and Florentine and Isa loaded their cases into the boot. They headed for the motorway, got caught up in a monumental traffic jam and stared at the queue of vehicles crawling **bumper**-to-bumper for as far as they could see. They listened to the traffic reports on the radio, bit their fingernails, kept glancing at the time, and finally resigned themselves to missing the plane.

But they were in luck. They got to the airport without a second to spare. Inga wished them a happy holiday, and they ran to the check-in, panting heavily. When they got on the plane, they were **relieved** to see that they weren't the last. They found their seats, stowed their jackets in the overhead lockers and shoved their bags under the seats in front. And then the last remaining passenger turned up. She didn't just arrive; she really made an entrance.

"Wow!" said Isa. "I've never seen anyone like that before."

"Me neither …" Even Florentine – who had a fair-

---

to volunteer – sich freiwillig melden;
bumper – Stoßstange; relieved – erleichtert;
wacky – verrückt/skurril

ly **wacky dress sense** and often wore bright colours in her hair and on her lips and nails – was impressed by the newcomer, who was still standing next to the stewardess, enjoying the sensation she was creating.

She was slim, very tall, and had long honey-coloured hair styled in tight **ringlets** like a duchess. She was wearing a tight black top and a pair of **skin-tight** leather trousers with bright green braces. She made sure everyone had the chance to take a good look at her, before letting the stewardess guide her to her seat.

"Who on earth is that?" wondered Florentine. "And why isn't she flying first-class? She doesn't look like she belongs here."

"I expect first-class was sold out," said Isa. "Or maybe you can't get first-class on charter flights."

"Oh, who cares, I don't suppose we'll ever have to see her again. Well, are you looking forward to our island holiday?"

Isa thought for a moment. "Err … not yet," she said truthfully. "But maybe I will be soon."

Florentine nodded. "That's how I feel too."

They sat in silence.

As the plane taxied down the runway the airstewardesses lined up to demonstrate how to put on a life-jacket and where to find the exits, describing all kinds of useful things that, in the event of an emergency, would have to be done with a clear head and maximum speed. Then, once they were up in the air, it was time for the **refreshments**.

---

dress sense – Sinn für Mode; ringlets – Locken;
skintight – hauteng; refreshments – Erfrischungen

Florentine ordered a gin and tonic, then a second one and soon afterwards a third. She kept staring at the couple sitting across the **aisle** from them.

"Is something wrong?" Isa finally asked her.

Florentine jumped. She fished out her trendy rucksack from under the seat in front and rummaged through it in search of some tissues.

"Don't worry … it's nothing," said Florentine, blowing her nose.

Isa checked the time. What would her parents be doing right now? They must have finished packing, and were probably loading their bags into the car. Isa grinned. Her dad would usually be shouting at this point, because he couldn't understand why one person should need so many clothes, **toiletries** and other stuff for just a few days away.

And what would Paul be doing? He'd be in his element, putting up the tent and making a fire, playing with his friends at being pioneers and adventurers.

Would Felix be taking care of Astra? Felix and Astra. Thinking of them made Isa feel almost **homesick**. No, not homesick exactly, thought Isa critically; it was more a kind of **longing**. What a dreadful word – longing! Oh well, it was only a week, after all. She'd always got on well with Florentine, she was looking forward to meeting new people, and everything else would take care of itself. Isa pulled a magazine from her rucksack and **immersed** herself in the moving story of an ageing **celebrity**.

---

aisle – Gang; toiletries – Toilettenartikel;
to feel homesick – Heimweh haben; longing – Sehnsucht;
to immerse – sich vertiefen; celebrity – Prominente(r)

After a while she laughed out loud. "Listen to this, Florentine. See what they've written about this guy: 'He's like a croissant – you can fill him with almost anything, but in the end he's just hot air!' What do you think of that? Not bad, huh?"

There was no response.

Isa raised her head and looked at her aunt in horror. "Are you feeling sick or something?"

Florentine was crying.

"What's up? What's wrong with you? Are you in pain?"

Florentine shook her head and carried on crying.

"Come on, you can tell me ..." Isa pulled a fresh tissue from the packet and handed it to her aunt. "No one cries without a reason. So what's wrong?"

"Look ... those two ... over there ..." sobbed Florentine, jabbing her chin in the direction of the couple, who were kissing with amazing **stamina**.

"Does it bother you, the two of them **snogging**?" asked Isa in surprise. "That kind of thing doesn't usually get to you."

"It's not getting to me, it's just that ... that ... well, sometimes I still think of ... you know who, and when I see couples like that, it's all a bit much for me and ..." Florentine sobbed again.

"So because of your wretched ex, you're trying to drown us all," said Isa. "I can't say that I'm following your logic. You should be pleased **to be shot of him**."

"I am pleased ..."

"Well then ..."

---

stamina – Durchhaltevermögen; to snog – rumknutschen;
to be shot of sb – jmd. los sein

"But I could do with another **G&T**. Do me a favour and call the trolley for me."

"I think three G&Ts will do," said Isa. "I've got a sip of coke here – how about that?"

"Thanks," said Florentine, wiping her eyes.

Isa was bored of reading about the ageing celeb. She slid the magazine into the pouch on the seat in front and looked out of the window. There wasn't much to see apart from the clouds, but they came in such amazing shapes that she just kept watching, casting a sideways glance towards Florentine every now and then.

**Lovesick**, she thought, so that's what it's like to be lovesick. It clearly knocked you right off balance. It wasn't long ago that Florentine had told them that she was over it, and had taken them out to dinner in celebration. But it was obvious how wrong she'd been – just the sight of two people kissing and she was **back to square one**. Hopefully, thought Isa, hopefully, there'll be loads to do in the resort so she won't have time to look at other people and think of Bert-Wolfram. Maybe after an action-packed week she'll have trouble remembering who he is. And maybe, just maybe, she'll even meet another man. That would be the best solution. How long does it take to **recover from** lovesickness? A week, a month, a year – or even longer? It all depended on the relationship. Isa sighed and glanced at Florentine. She was asleep at last.

---

G&T – gin and tonic; to be lovesick – Liebeskummer haben; to be back to square one – wieder da sein, wo man angefangen hat; to recover from sth – sich von etw. erholen

Isa took the sick-bag out of the pouch and filled it with used tissues.

How could Florentine be pleased and still start crying ... ? **Beats me,** she thought. The alcohol didn't seem to have helped. I'll have to take good care of my aunt in future ...

Isa had to laugh.

---

Beats me! – Das versteh ich nicht!

## Beach Club on the Med

As she got off the plane, Isa realized in surprise that it was **barely** warmer on the island than it had been at home. True, the Mediterranean sun was beating down from the cloudless blue sky, but the wind swept **mercilessly** through the thin fabric of her T-shirt.

They hurried into the airport, collected their luggage from the conveyor belt and made their way to the exit, where their arrival had been anticipated. Written in fancy letters on a kind of flag were the words: "Welcome to the beach club!"

"That's where we're headed!" said Florentine. "Hello … I think we're part of your group, Mrs … ?"

"Welcome!" **beamed** the young woman standing next to the flag.

"She's seen one too many adverts for toothpaste," whispered Isa to her aunt. "Just you wait and see, in a moment her teeth will start glinting."

"Shush … Don't get yourself a reputation already." Florentine pushed her suitcase to one side. "Were you waiting for us?"

"For you and the rest of your group," said the woman. She still hadn't stopped beaming. "My

---

barely – kaum; mercilessly – gnadenlos;
to beam – vor Freude strahlen

name's Bridget, by the way. We're all on first-name terms in the resort. And you are …?"

"Florentine," replied Florentine reluctantly.

Bridget **skimmed** through her list, glanced at Isa, and checked the list again. Her smile looked distinctly less radiant. She turned to Isa. "Someone must have made a mistake. You're clearly not Bert-Wolfram, are you?"

Florentine's not going to like that question, thought Isa in alarm. She put her arm **protectively** around her aunt.

Florentine gulped. "Too right. 'Bert-Wolfram' was a terrible mistake, but I'd rather not talk about that now. This is Isa, my niece."

"Welcome to the island, Isa," said Bridget, her smile restored.

It was only then that Isa and Florentine noticed that they weren't the only ones headed for the beach club. The two **lovebirds** were there, plus a few other people they'd seen on the plane, not to mention the woman with the lurid green braces.

"What did I tell you?" whispered Florentine. "You'll be able to write an amazing article …"

Finally Bridget managed to match the names on her list to the people gathered around her.

"Let's go!" she said, waving the flag as she walked towards the **coach**.

Of course it wasn't just an ordinary coach; it was an extravagantly colourful vehicle designed to make the world a brighter, livelier place. The passengers in-

---

to skim sth – etw. überfliegen; protectively – schützend; Lovebirds – „Turteltauben"; coach – Reisebus side it *seemed* cheery enough, although, thought Isa, some of them actually *looked* a bit **dreary** with their check trousers, colour-coordinated polo shirts and grey faces ...

But there was a group of teenagers of about her age at the back, laughing and joking around. She would have liked to have joined them, but that wasn't on – it wouldn't have been fair on Florentine.

The coach pulled away with a crunching of gears.

After about an hour's drive they turned off the main road, zigzagging down the hill. The coach put on a spurt of speed, sounded its horn and braked abruptly in front of an imposing **gate**. On either side of the gate were clusters of people in bikinis and boardshorts, smiling just like Bridget. They were clapping and shouting words of welcome.

"Are they talking to us?" asked a **portly**-looking lady.

"I expect so," said the man sitting next to her, pushing past Isa as he rushed to the door.

"Oi!" shouted Isa, taken aback. "Don't mind me!"

The man took no notice of her. He had already got his camera in position and was busy taking snaps of the **reception** committee.

"What a loser," exclaimed Florentine in a loud voice. "Men like that catch one glimpse of a bikini and go completely mad. You should write this down, Isa: never trust a man who **raves about** bikinis."

"Oh Florentine, you're impossible!" said Isa equally loudly. She quickly took some pictures of the

---

dreary – trostlos; gate – Tor; portly – korpulent;
reception – Empfang; to rave about sth – von etw. schwärmen

man taking pictures. She was glad Florentine's mood was improving. Maybe we'll have some fun this week after all, she hoped.

"Excuse me ..." said the portly woman indignantly.

The clapping finally died down.

In the foyer there were some pinkish-coloured drinks for the new arrivals.

"Do they contain alcohol?" asked someone.

"I hope so," said the portly woman's husband.

It turned out to be sickly-sweet juice. Isa took one sip and pulled a face. She put her glass back down.

Then someone told them what a wonderful group they were and how they were going to have an amazing time. Their keys were ready for collection and their luggage had been taken on ahead. "Dinner has already started, but not to worry, you can take your time."

"How long?" asked one of the lovebirds in a break between kisses.

"Until ten."

"That will do ..."

Isa cast a worried look towards Florentine. She was clutching the key and didn't seem to have heard. "We're in 'Red Rose', a bungalow with a **sea view**," she said. She watched the couple walk away and **vanish** around the corner. She took a deep breath and blew her nose.

"Come on, we've had enough tears for one day," said Isa energetically. "Let's go and check out our rooms."

---

sea view – Meerblick; to vanish – verschwinden

They set off together.

The light was already starting to fade. They turned right and then left, then straight on and right again … They seemed to be lost in some kind of labyrinth. Twice they found themselves faced with a dead end. They weren't sure whether to find it funny or annoying. Then at last they were standing in front of their bungalow, "Red Rose 13".

"Hang on a minute," said Florentine. "Where are our suitcases?"

"I guess they haven't got here yet," said Isa impatiently. "Here, give me the key."

She pushed it into the lock and twisted. Funny, it felt as though the door hadn't been closed properly. Isa shrugged, pushed it open, and **gestured** Florentine ahead. "After you."

She stepped aside to let Florentine past and then followed her into the bungalow.

They were standing in the hall. White tiles covered the floor. To the left the bathroom door was open, so you could see straight in. To the right were fitted cupboards and a mirror stretching up to the ceiling. A few steps led up to the living room, which had a small sofa, two armchairs and a table. On the table was a vase of red roses along with two wine-glasses and a bottle.

A candle was burning.

"What a great welcome present," said Isa.

"Wine, flowers and a ca…"

She had been meaning to say candle, but she couldn't get the word out in time.

---

to gesture sb somewhere – jmd. wohin winken

A man had appeared around the corner and was standing in the dim light in front of them. He was just as surprised as Florentine and Isa. And he wasn't wearing any clothes.

He was **stark naked**.

For a few moments they stood frozen to the spot, with just the candlelight flickering.

"What the hell …?" said the man.

Florentine **shrieked** and rushed towards the door.

"Sorry," stammered Isa and stumbled after her.

The door banged behind them. They were back outside again. They clutched each other's hands and exchanged looks. Everything was quiet.

Then all of a sudden Florentine buried her face in her hands and started crying uncontrollably.

Oh no, thought Isa. "What's the matter now?" she asked.

"It wasn't … Oh, you know …" sobbed Florentine. "It wasn't him. And if it had been …" She sniffed.

"But you were the one who **sent** him **packing**," said Isa in astonishment. "And it was you who told him never to come back. So what exactly do you want?"

"I know, I know," wept Florentine. "But even so … If he hadn't been such a lying cheat then I wouldn't have had to send him packing, and then he'd be here, and …"

"And I'd still be at home, revising my maths," said Isa coldly.

---

stark naked – splitterfasernackt; to shriek – schreien;
to send sb packing – jmd. wegschicken

"I'm not criticizing you," Florentine rushed to reassure her. She sniffed and rummaged through her rucksack for a tissue.

Isa looked around. They were the only ones about. Everyone else was in the dining-hall – except for the naked man. She giggled. She'd definitely be using that in her article. It's not every day you see something like that. If she told the story to Felix or her friends they would think she was making it up.

Florentine sniffed again. "What's so **hilarious**? Are you laughing at me?"

"You have to see the funny side," giggled Isa. "The flickering candlelight as he came around the corner ..." She was laughing again. Florentine laughed too.

Back at reception the mystery was solved. Earlier that afternoon the computer had crashed, muddling up all the records. Their bungalow was "Red Rose 31", and that's where their cases were waiting.

They got changed, brushed their hair and headed towards the dining-hall at last. Isa's stomach was **rumbling**, but she had high hopes for the evening.

They walked through a maze of little paths until they reached a kind of square. From there they could see an enormous, brightly-lit building. Music was coming from inside, and you could hear the clatter of plates, the chinking of glasses and the **hubbub** of voices. Kids were racing around, playing hide-and-seek or jumping noisily into the pool. That's what I call a holiday atmosphere, thought Isa in satisfaction.

---

hubbub – Lärm, Stimmengewirr; hilarious – urkomisch; to rumble – knurren

It's exactly how I'd imagined it to be. I bet there's plenty going on here!

"Look at all these awful people," said Florentine in a gloomy voice. "They're absolutely **revolting**. How can anyone put up with them? Big groups just aren't my thing. I'm going back. I'm not hungry now anyway. I've completely lost my appetite."

"Rubbish. Things won't seem half as bad when you've eaten." Isa dragged her aunt with her in the direction of the entrance.

An enormous buffet had been laid out with salads, fish, slices of meat, mountains of pasta, heaps of rice and piles of potatoes. "Maybe I am hungry after all," said Florentine, as they strolled past the food. "Do me a favour and find a little table just for the two of us, would you?"

"I'll give it a go ..."

Isa couldn't see any tables for two. The best she could find was a table for six with no one sitting around it.

She reserved two places and **wandered** back to the buffet.

"Hi," said someone standing next to her.

Isa turned round and smiled. "Hi. So you're here too."

"Yeah." He was messing around with his plate in embarrassment. "I saw you on the plane. Your hair is ... really wacky. And ... ," he pointed to her fingers, "I couldn't help noticing your nails."

Isa laughed. "Watch out!" she warned him, "you've got vinaigrette dripping from your plate."

---

revolting – ekelhaft; to wander – schlendern

"Thanks," he said.
"No problem."
Neither of them said anything. They looked at each other, grinning.
"How long are you here for?"
"A week. How about you?"
"Me too. Did you come with your parents?"
Isa shook her head. "No, with my aunt."
"Hmm ... Sounds like you **drew the short straw**."
"Not really," said Isa. "She's usually really cool ... And you? Here with your parents, being a good son?"
"I'm with my dad."
"Oh."
"What's your name?"
"Isa. And yours?"
"Jannik."
"God, what a name," joked Isa.
"I can't help my parents' taste."
"That's true ... Well, in any case, I'm hungry. Take care."
"Will I see you again?" asked Jannik. "It's a pretty big place."
"So you've looked around already?"
Jannik nodded. "What do you say then?"
Isa looked at her plate. "I haven't even had a chance to eat yet."
"Is there room for me and my dad on your table?"
Isa was about to say yes, but then remembered Florentine. "My aunt isn't really **in the mood**. Sorry, but I think she's just tired."

---

to draw the short straw – den Kürzeren ziehen;
not to be in the mood – schlecht gelaunt sein

“OK. I’ll call round in an hour then. Where’s your room?”

“Red Rose 31,” Isa told him reluctantly. “Are you always this direct?”

Jannik laughed. “Only to you!”

“God and you’re **slimy** with it!”

“Yup. So I’ll drop by in an hour then.”

“Can’t promise I’ll be there.”

“I’ll risk it.”

Isa looked at him. The sun had gone down ages ago, but he was still wearing sunglasses with little round **lenses**. His hair was shaved close to his head, and the bit he had left glowed a carroty-orange colour.

Isa laughed. “Well, it’s certainly not boring here. First I come face to face with a man **in the nude** and now you. It looks like it’s going to be an exciting week.”

“A man in the nude?” echoed Jannik, frowning. He tugged on his baggy shorts. “I don’t follow. Come again?”

“Later,” said Isa, turning away. Then she spun around to face him: “And **watch out**, you’re dripping vinaigrette again. Too bad for your fancy shirt.”

“Sh...” he cursed. “But about your nails – do they always look that crazy?”

Isa was taken aback. “Well, naturally. Anything to stand out from the **crowd**! But you’re sliming again. I actually just collect nail varnish.”

By the time Isa got back to the table, Florentine had already emptied half a bottle of wine. A few bits of

---

slimy – schleimig; lens – Glas (für Brillen); in the nude – nackt; Watch out! – Vorsicht!; crowd – (Menschen-)Masse

lettuce were swimming in some leftover sauce. A piece of half-eaten bread lay **abandoned** next to the plate. Her aunt was sitting there, chin resting on her hands, staring at the ceiling **morosely**.

Isa laughed to herself. "Someone's dropping by for me later. You don't mind, do you?"

"Of course not," said Florentine and reached for the bottle.

"Have some water," Isa recommended. "It's healthier."

"Not for me it isn't," replied Florentine. "So who are you meeting up with?"

"He's called Jannik. He was on the same plane as us. He asked if he could sit here, but I knew you didn't want to be **disturbed**. Maybe I can point him out ..."

While she was eating, she kept an eye out for Jannik, but she couldn't see him anywhere. Right next to them, though, was a table of teenagers of about her own age. They were screaming with laughter, yelling at each other, waving their **cutlery** around and flapping their arms wildly. Isa watched them wistfully. At least they were enjoying themselves ... Typical – her first evening on the island and she was lumbered with the gloomiest person in the room. What had she done to **deserve** that?

But tomorrow, tomorrow would be different. She'd make sure that she got to know the bunch at the other table. Since she'd been forced to come on holi-

---

abandoned – verlassen; morosely – mürrisch;
to disturb – stören; cutlery – Besteck;
to deserve – verdienen

day in the first place, she was **determined** to have a good time. And to experience as much as possible and write an amazing article!

She must have been looking at them with obvious envy. A girl with tanned skin and blonde hair waved at her and called something out.

"What?" Isa yelled, trying to make herself heard above the noise.

The others laughed, but it was a friendly-sounding laugh. The girl was shouting something again. It sounded Spanish or Italian, in any case a language that Isa's school had failed to teach her.

"Hello," said a voice right beside her. "You don't mind if I join you, do you?"

It was the duchess from the plane. The leather trousers and neon-green braces were gone, replaced by a **sequined** body and the tiniest mini skirt that Isa had ever seen. But there was no mistaking her height and her splendid mop of curls.

"My name's Tersia," she said, sliding elegantly onto the chair. "I remember the two of you from the plane and the coach. How long are you staying for?"

"A week," said Florentine, reluctant to be drawn.

"Perfect," replied Tersia **cheerily**. "I'm only here for a week as well. Gosh, I'm starving. Bon appetit!"

With any luck they'll get on well together, thought Isa. If the two of them make friends, everything will be sorted: Florentine will be taken care of, and I'll be free to do as I please. She looked over to the other table again.

---

determined – entschlossen; sequined – mit Pailletten besetzt; cheerily – fröhlich

"Want to join us?" yelled one of the girls.

"Well, go on then," said Florentine. "Make the most of the evening, but take care of yourself, all right? And don't stay up too late."

Tersia laughed. "So what are you, her big sister? You're definitely not old enough to be her mum!"

"Too right," said Florentine. "Isa's my niece. She's here because ..." Florentine fell silent.

"Because we get on so well," Isa interjected. "So she **treated** me **to** a whole week's holiday abroad. Amazing, huh?" She got up. "Bye Florentine, and don't worry about me, OK?"

One of the girls at the other table moved over and offered Isa the other half of her chair.

One of the boys asked: "Got here today, did you? I can tell from the colour of your skin. You're still **pale** as anything. Where do you come from?"

"Germany," said Isa. "How about you?"

"Switzerland. My name's Nico." He pointed to the girl sitting on the other half of Isa's seat: "That's Amelie, my sister. And what's your name?"

Isa introduced herself.

"Want to come along? We're off to the clubhouse, that's where all the action is. Carlos does the best **mime** show in the entire world. He'll crack you up," said Nico.

Isa looked at the others questioningly.

"Haven't you heard? There's always a show in the evenings. The guys that work here are performers. We always go along to watch or even join in, depending."

---

to treat sb to sth – jmd. zu etw. einladen/jmd. etw. spendieren; pale – blass; mime – Pantomime

"How long does it last?" asked Isa, thinking of Florentine.

"Right through the night," said Nico. "Well, you didn't come here to sleep, did you? Or at least not to sleep like at home: clothes off, crawl into bed, light out, snore."

Everyone laughed.

"Yeah, of course, I'll come along." Isa was looking forward to it. It was bound to be a laugh. "I'm just going back to grab a **sweater**. I'll catch you later."

She'd forgotten about Jannik.

This time Isa only took one wrong turn on her way to Red Rose 31. She congratulated herself on her cleverness and was just unlocking the door, pulling and pushing to jerk it open, when she noticed someone sitting on the floor.

"Christ," yelled Isa. "Don't make me jump like that!"

"I've been here for so long I must have fallen asleep," explained Jannik. He stood up and propped something against the wall. "My skateboard," he said.

"Hang on a minute ..." Isa disappeared into the bungalow. "Want to come with me to the clubhouse?" she shouted from inside. "I've met a few people and I'm joining them there." Isa pulled the sweater over her head and slammed the door behind her. "So, are you coming or not?"

"Have you been out onto the **patio** in front of your bungalow yet?" asked Jannik, without answering her question. "Here, give me the key and I'll show you."

Isa was so taken aback that she handed him the key.

---

sweater – Pullover; patio – Terrasse

When they got to the patio, she shrieked: "Hey! What's all this about? I don't like **being ambushed**!"

"OK, OK," Jannik soothed her. "Why don't we sit down over here?"

He was right: the patio did look pretty. Something flowery and sweet-smelling was poking its **tendrils** through the lattices of the little wooden roof that sheltered a table and some chairs. And there was a little wall that you could sit on and **gaze** out over the sea.

"It's about the naked man," said Jannik by way of apology. "You're going to have to tell me about it. Was he a **flasher**? You know, the type that walks around with nothing under his coat, scaring young girls. Was he lying in wait for you? Did he say anything to you? Tell me what he said."

"What the hell ...!"

"Was it really that bad?" asked Jannik with feeling. "That's terrible. It must have been a real shock. What did he look like?"

Isa was back in control. "What did he look like? No idea. I was too surprised to take any notice."

Jannik nodded, "If you ask me, men like that are absolute **scum**. They're lower than the lowest of the low ... I just thought, if you could maybe describe him to me, I could ..."

"Could what?"

"Could sort him out for you," said Jannik resolutely.

"You're all man!"

---

to be ambushed – aus dem Hinterhalt überfallen werden; tendril – Ranke; to gaze – schauen; flasher – Exhibitionist; scum – Abschaum;

Jannik realized that Isa was teasing him. "You're taking it very lightly," he said disapprovingly. "You're not that **unscrupulous** already, are you?"

"Why shouldn't I be?" laughed Isa. "Don't worry, I don't need rescuing. It wasn't like that at all."

"Well, how was it then?"

"We were given the key to the wrong bungalow, someone was in there already, and when we unlocked the door, a naked man walked around the corner. That's all."

"Oh, OK then." Jannik sounded really disappointed. "Well, I guess we should go."

---

unscrupulous – abgebrüht

# Nightlife

Crowds of trendily-dressed happy people were packed into the clubhouse and **milling around** in front of the doors. Isa saw **the height of** sportswear **fashion**, all kinds of swish dresses and men wearing cotton shirts, now beautifully ironed. The smell of shampoo filled the air.

The pool was lit-up, someone was singing into a microphone, people were strolling past or standing around in groups, chatting and laughing. Everyone seemed determined to have a good time.

All of a sudden, Amelie appeared in front of them, grabbed Isa by the arm and pulled her into the clubhouse – the music made it impossible to communicate in any other way. Someone pressed a bottle of coke into Isa's hand and pointed towards the stage: a man in a black dinner jacket, white shirt, red **bow-tie**, face as white as chalk and thick black eyebrows was sitting on a chair, reading the newspaper.

A **fly** settled on one of his hands. He brushed it away and carried on reading. It circled above his head. He looked up in irritation. The fly walked over his newspaper. That really got to him. He shook the

---

to mill around – umherlaufen; the height of fashion – nach der neuesten Mode; bow-tie – Fliege (Kleidungsstück); fly – Fliege (Insekt)

paper and a few sheets came loose, fluttering to the ground. He sighed, bent down and picked them up, piece by piece. He tried to put them in the right order – he liked to keep things tidy – but dropped the whole thing on the floor.

The fly landed on his nose. He sniffed. It moved to his forehead. He got up, knelt down and picked up the pages one by one … The fly was enjoying the game. It **swooped** and twisted, following his movements as it helped him to collect the sheets.

The man had no sense of humour. He didn't find the fly in the least bit funny. He stopped picking up the paper and seized one sheet. He folded it and waited for the fly.

The fly stopped short. It was a **worldly-wise** insect with plenty of experience of humans. When the man lunged forwards to attack, it looped around his head, beat its wings in a cheeky little wave and flew away.

The onlookers were bent double with laughter, but the man was deeply disappointed.

His arm hung loosely by his side as he dangled his paper weapon. He seemed utterly **dejected**: no hunt, no battle and no victory – what a sorry tale …

"That's what happens when you stop communicating and start to grow apart," said a man to his companion.

Isa turned in the direction of the voice. It belonged to an elderly gentleman. The woman walking beside him was much younger. She was wearing the usual lit-

---

to swoop – herabstoßen; worldly-wise – weltklug; dejected – niedergeschlagen tle black dress, had the usual long blonde hair and was chewing gum and looking bored.

Isa watched them walk away and **swore** never to be like them. But as a reporter things were bound to be more exciting, she thought, and she joined in the applause.

Amelie, Isa, Jannik and Nico pulled over some chairs and sat in a group by the pool.

They'd only just got settled when Nico **pointed to** a girl. "That's Senta. I know her from water-skiing."

"So what do you guys get up to all day?" asked Isa.

"All day?" echoed Nico. "We don't have all day; we only have half."

Isa laughed. "Really? How come?"

"Well, we have to make sure we get our sleep, so we stay in bed till lunch-time. Then we drag ourselves off to get something to eat. And then, if everything's going to plan, we meet up at the **jetty** where Hugo and the water-skiing instructors hang out – the three of them can teach you how to handle the skis and the water."

Isa suddenly thought of Felix. What would he think about people who talked about "handling" a horse? And what would he think of Jannik's hair, his baggy skater-clothes and the sunglasses he never seemed to take off. Or of Nico and staying in bed until midday? Felix was completely different, Isa **concluded**.

Senta interrupted her thoughts. "But in the evening we've got bags of energy. Come on, guys, my feet are **itching**. Want to dance?"

---

to swear – schwören; to point to sth – auf etw. zeigen;
jetty – Pier; to conclude – beschließen; to itch – jucken

The nightclub looked no different to any of the other clubs that Isa knew from home, but the atmosphere was totally different: less serious, more **casual**, more holiday-like, she thought.

She would have liked to stand to one side and jot down some observations and impressions for the article. Photos would have been useful too – that way she could describe everyone when she got back home. But she soon forgot the idea. There was no chance of peace and quiet with the others around.

She **lost track** of time, and it was only when her neck and feet started to ache that she looked at her watch. It was two in the morning. Suddenly she felt dead tired and longed to be in bed.

It was pitch-black in the bungalow.

She got undressed in the bathroom and even managed to go through her usual bedtime ritual, washing her face and cleaning her teeth.

She tried to find her bed in the dark. After all, Florentine was sleeping.

At the sound of Florentine's voice she jumped in surprise.

"God, you startled me," said Isa. "Have you only just got home?"

"No, I've been here a while. Been enjoying yourself?"

Isa **yawned**. "I've had a great time. I met a few people, and they're really OK." Isa yawned again. "Do you know how to water-ski, Florentine?"

---

casual – locker; to lose track of sth – etw. aus den Augen verlieren; to yawn – gähnen

"No, but I'm willing to learn."

"So how was your evening? Did you get on all right with curly-haired Tersia?"

"Yes, it was fine."

Florentine's voice didn't seem to be coming from her bed. Isa groped for the light-switch. "What's up with you?"

Her aunt was sitting wrapped in her **duvet** next to the open patio door.

"Don't you feel tired?" said Isa. "Don't you want to go to sleep?"

"I am tired and I do want to go to sleep, but I can't."

"Oh God ... you're not thinking about your ex again, are you? That dreadful guy ..."

Florentine didn't reply. Then she said quietly: "Right now I'm thinking about me. I'm rebelling against myself – against my blindness, about the way I chose to be blind and kept being blind ..."

"I don't follow. It's a bit too heavy for me right now." Isa yawned. "Can we talk about it once we've had some sleep?"

"We don't have to talk about it at all. It's my problem, and I have to learn how to deal with it."

"But I want to help you," said Isa sleepily, "just not right now. Come on, let's go to bed."

She was woken up by a noise. Reluctantly she opened her eyes, turned around and sat up.

It was already getting light in the room. The patio door was open and the curtain was blowing in the **breeze**.

---

duvet – Daunendecke; breeze – Brise

The bed next to her was empty.

"Florentine?" Isa couldn't hear her. She'd probably just gone to the toilet.

Isa snuggled back under the covers and was about to go to sleep. But I haven't heard the **flush**, she thought. If Florentine is in the toilet, I should be able to hear the flush. But I haven't heard anything. Sh…

Isa crawled out of bed. The bathroom was empty.

She walked **barefoot** through the room and out onto the patio. Nothing.

The beach club's boats and catamarans were tied up on the shore.

The beach was deserted. Little waves advanced towards the shore, ran back and darted forwards again. There was something very soothing about the movement; it made Isa want to fall asleep.

The sun wasn't up yet. A thin layer of mist hung over the sea.

Isa yawned. Florentine is old enough to look after herself, she thought. She's my aunt. If she wants to go for an early morning walk, that's up to her … Maybe she's jogging along the beach, enjoying being on her own without anyone else around her. And why shouldn't she?

She went back to bed, pulled the duvet over her head, closed her eyes and was nearly asleep when she suddenly remembered their late-night chat.

What had Florentine said? "I'm rebelling against myself …" If she'd have said that she was "annoyed" with herself, Isa wouldn't have thought twice about it. But "rebelling"? That sounded serious.

---

flush – Spülung; barefoot – barfüßig

Rebels were fighters; people who refused to sit back and accept things; people who spoke out and acted. All well and good, thought Isa, but you can't fight against nothing. You need an **opponent**.

Her mind was racing. If you rebel against yourself, you're the person fighting and the person being fought against. That must be terrible.

She rolled over and rested her head on her arm. That's **the pits**, she thought. No matter how hard you fight, one half of you is always destined to lose. And the other half wins. What good does that do? Not a bit. Half a victory is no victory at all, she decided. It's a bit like being **pregnant**: you're either pregnant or you're not. You either win or you don't.

But is that really true? she asked herself critically. No, she thought, not exactly. A fight can sometimes **end in a draw**.

What happens when you fight yourself and it's a draw?

Isa gazed at the ceiling, thinking hard.

It must be dreadful; the absolute worst. You're not going forwards or backwards – you feel like a mouse in a **trap** ... It's easier in football, she thought. In football you just keep shooting penalties until one of them lands in the goal. Then the match is over, and the winning team goes home happy, while the losers leave dejected.

That's how it works in football.

But what about Florentine?

---

opponent – Gegner; to be the pits – das Letzte sein;
pregnant – schwanger; to end in a draw – unentschieden enden;
trap – Falle

Isa yawned. She'd have to ask her, when she was back.

When would that be?

All of a sudden, Isa was **wide awake**.

I can't just lie here mumbling to myself, she thought. I've got to do something. I've got to find Florentine and help her through this. Isa leapt out of bed, put on some jeans, socks, shoes and a sweater, and set off.

First she turned right out of the bungalow and walked along the beach until she got to a little cabin. There was a man dressed in uniform **snoozing** inside.

"Have you seen a lady walk past?" she asked him.

He shook his head.

So Isa retraced her steps and took a quick look inside the bungalow, just in case Florentine had **reappeared**. She hadn't.

So Isa went back outside, turned left past the boats and carried on until she got to a little mound. At the summit were some scattered ruins and ancient columns, now **overgrown** with olive trees and shrubs.

That was where she found Florentine. She was sitting on an upturned column, leaning against an olive tree and gazing out over the sea. She looked so sad and lonely that Isa would have liked to pick her up and hug her like a child.

She sat down next to her.

After a while she said softly: "Can't you just stop letting it get to you?"

---

wide awake – hellwach;
to snooze – ein Nickerchen machen; to reappear – wieder auftauchen; overgrown – überwuchert

"I wish I could, but I can't. Right now I feel like a detective who's found a **trail** and has followed it until it divides in two. And now I'm standing here, looking at the different paths and wondering how it happened." Florentine fell silent.

"Well, carry on then, how did it happen?"

"You know," said Florentine, "if you really love someone, you trust them. You can't have love without trust; it's like the left and right shoes of a pair. You trust the person you love and you see in his eyes whether he loves you and whether he trusts you in return."

"But you and Bert-Wolfram, you trusted each other, didn't you?" probed Isa.

Florentine nodded. "For a while everything was fine."

"And then, what happened?"

Florentine rubbed her eyes and shook her head. "It's a pretty horrible feeling when you realize someone likes to have your trust but isn't giving anything in return. You feel like ... like ... like a small child who's been given a **bucket and spade** and sent to play in the **sandpit**: 'Run along and play!'"

Isa nodded. "I know what you mean. I still remember how seriously I used to take my mud pies. 'Baking' in the garden was an important part of my life back then! But when I showed my parents, they never paid any attention. They thought it was a game, of course. I understand that now, but it really got to me at the time."

---

trail – Spur; bucket and spade – Eimer und Schaufel;
sandpit – Sandkasten

Florentine laughed. "Well, I guess you know how I feel then."

"So when did you notice that Bert-Wolfram wasn't taking you seriously; that he was letting you play in the sandpit?"

Florentine shrugged and got up. "I'm not sure exactly … I couldn't tell you, not yet. Come on, let's go back. The first bathers are about to take the plunge. And the joggers are out and about too."

After a few metres Florentine stopped. "Listen, Isa, I don't want you to worry about me. I want you to enjoy yourself, to do whatever you want. It really doesn't bother me if we only meet at mealtimes, OK?"

"Are you sure you can **manage**?"

"Course I can," said Florentine, trying to sound like she meant it.

---

to manage sth – mit etw. zurechtkommen

## Reconnaissance

Isa dreamt she was caught in a storm. She could distinctly hear the **threatening** roar of thunder. It went on and on, rattling and bellowing, until she was forced to open her eyes.

Florentine was standing in her dressing gown at the half-open door. She was talking to someone; but Isa couldn't see whom.

"But it's practically half-ten!" Isa knew that voice immediately – it belonged to Jannik. "No one can stay in bed for that long!"

"We can," said Florentine emphatically. "So don't even think of coming back before twelve. The last thing we need right now is stress. We **got rid** of our stress before we left home. We put it in a **bullet-proof case**, locked the lid and left it in the **vaults**!"

Isa grinned. Florentine was like that when she was happy. That's how Isa knew her. It was her stupid loser of a boyfriend who had turned her into a snivelling **wretch**. But Florentine seemed to be feeling a bit better at last.

"Whoa!" said Jannik. Isa could tell he didn't know whether or not Florentine was joking or whether

---

threatening – drohend; to get rid of sb/sth – jmd./etw. loswerden; bullet-proof case – kugelsicherer Koffer; vaults – Tresorraum; wretch – Miststück

she was completely and utterly mad. Maybe it was both.

He gave in. "Till twelve then," he said.

Florentine shut the door and came back to bed. "He's not afraid of wearing bright colours," she laughed. "And I don't know where he gets his clothes from, but it must be a shop for super-large sizes."

"Nah, he's just taken a growth pill, and he's waiting for it to work," said Isa cheerily. She leapt out of bed and fetched her collection of nail varnish. "Today I'm going for lime-green with silvery-blue dots," she announced. "As for Jannik, he's perfectly OK and everything, but he takes himself too seriously. I told him about the naked man, and he was all for calling the **vice squad**. He wanted to stand guard over me day and night to stop me getting into trouble."

Florentine giggled.

Applying the nail varnish was a tricky business, and Isa gave it her all. Her tongue kept poking out of her mouth as if it wanted to watch. Finally her nails were ready to be admired.

Isa grinned in satisfaction at the lime-green, silvery-blue artwork and shook her hands to dry the varnish.

For her toenails she took the easy option, painting the left foot lime-green and the right foot silvery-blue. She finished in no time. She jumped out of bed and looked in the mirror.

Oh no! Her hair! It was always the same: no matter how long she **combed** it for, it never made a difference. Isa had a shower and then got dressed – shorts, a green T-shirt and red hat. The hat would hide

---

vice squad – Sittenpolizei; to comb – kämmen

her hair at least. That was the best she could do for the moment. And then it was time to worry about Florentine.

Isa waited until her aunt **emerged** from the bathroom. Oh well, she thought critically, it could be worse.

Florentine stood in front of the full-length mirror, looking herself up and down. "Tomorrow I'll start making myself look more presentable," she decided. "If you look good, you feel more **confident**, and that makes you happier. You should make a note of that." She stuck her tongue out at her reflection.

"Yes, aunty Flo," said Isa dutifully. "Now hurry up, I'm dying of hunger – we haven't had anything to eat since yesterday."

"Aren't you going to wait for Jannik?"

"Jannik? Jannik who?" joked Isa. "We're bound to bump into him on the way."

"You're impossible," said Florentine. "When you make a promise, you have to keep it. Just look at me! Do you see what happens if you start relying on people who can't be trusted?"

"That's not fair," said Isa laughing. "You were wrong about your boyfriend, but I know exactly what Jannik's like – he's a self-important slime-ball. I don't want anything from him, I don't **expect** anything from him, and I haven't promised myself anything from him. And that, aunty Flo, is most important of all. Back home I've got Felix waiting for me, not to mention the others."

---

to emerge – herauskommen; confident – selbstbewusst; expect – erwarten

"You'll come to a bad end, you will," predicted Florentine. "Now, where the hell is our key? We can't go anywhere without it."

"Oh yes we can – I've got one too, remember? And if we don't eat now, I'm going to die of **starvation**."

There was a knock on the door.

"Jannik," said Florentine.

"He's a real pest," groaned Isa. "Oh. It's you," she said as she opened the door. "About time too, Jannik, we've been waiting for ages."

"B… b… but your aunt told me …"

"OK, OK. Just hurry up – it's time for lunch!"

"My key!" shouted Florentine. "I'm still looking for my key!" She lifted a mound of clothes from the chair, took her handbag off the table, and searched her bed, the floor and the bathroom. The key was nowhere to be found.

In the end, Isa and Jannik joined in the hunt, and it was Jannik who finally found it. Well, at least he can do something apart from getting on my nerves, thought Isa.

In the dining hall another magnificent buffet had been laid out. Walking past the food **made** Isa's **mouth water** in bucket-loads.

Nico and Amelie waved at them from the other side of the room. They'd saved them a place at their table.

"Want to join us Florentine?" asked Isa half-heartedly.

---

starvation – Hungertod; it makes her mouth water – das lässt ihr das Wasser im Mund zusammenlaufen

"I'm not that stupid," said her aunt. She took a look around the room and smiled **in relief**. "I'm going to sit with Tersia. I'll see you later, OK?"

"What's wrong with your aunt?" asked Jannik. "She looked really odd this morning – as if she'd been crying or something. She was in a bad mood yesterday too. Is something the matter?"

Isa nodded. "Yeah, she's in a bad way. There's this **bloke** that she used to live with, but she's just sent him packing because ... because ... well, it's none of your business really. In any case, she's still ..." Isa hesitated.

"Heartbroken" was what she'd been thinking, but it sounded so old-fashioned that she couldn't bring herself to say it.

Jannik nodded sympathetically. "And now she's got **withdrawal symptoms**. I know how it is from my dad. I'm the poor **substitute** for his ex-girlfriend."

"Really?" Isa stopped abruptly. "Hang on a minute. So your dad's single, and so is Florentine. Why don't we pair them up? Then they'll both be happy and everything will be taken care of. And we wouldn't have to worry about them any more."

"I thought of that yesterday too. We should give it a go – it might work and it might not. We'd just have to set them up and see."

"Great! So how shall we do it?"

"Does your aunt play tennis?" asked Jannik.

"Not very often, so not very well."

"Hmm. That's no good then."

---

in relief – erleichtert; bloke – Kerl; withdrawal symptoms – Entzugserscheinungen; substitute – Ersatz

Isa thought for a moment. "I think the best thing would be to introduce them at dinner," she said at last. "You know, without **making** any **fuss**. You'd just go, 'Hi Isa, this is my dad', and I'd say, 'Oh hi Jannik. This is my aunt'. What do you reckon?"

Jannik rested his sunglasses on his orange-coloured stubbly hair. "It might work. We'd have to do it naturally, otherwise they'd **guess** we were up to something and then we'd be for it."

Nico ate plate-loads of spaghetti and burgers; he refused to eat anything else. The others stuffed themselves on salad, chips and all kinds of vegetables, and **took the mickey out of** Nico, who carried on eating **undeterred**. In fact, he even went back for more. To finish off they all **shovelled** down glacier-sized portions of ice cream, and then proclaimed themselves fit for fun, life and water-skiing.

Nico, Amelie, Senta, Jannik and Isa wandered down to the jetty together. Some middle-aged people had been sunbathing there, but they soon **retreated** when Isa and the others pushed their way forwards. They sat on the edge, legs dangling in the water, spraying each other.

"That's the best way of getting rid of the crowds," said Amelie.

"What's the big deal?" asked Isa.

"You'll soon see ... Look! The boats are on their

---

to make a fuss – einen Aufstand machen; to guess – erraten;
to take the mickey out of sb – jmd. veräppeln;
undeterred – nicht abgeschreckt; to shovel – schaufeln;
to retreat – sich zurückziehen

way!" said Amelie. She got up, waved and yelled across the water. "Yoo-hoo, Hugo, over here!"

Hugo steered the boat **expertly** towards the jetty, smiled his beach club smile and allowed Amelie to hug him.

He put his arm around her **patronizingly**: "Hi sweetie. You're looking wonderful as always. Compared to you, Julia Roberts is a computer-generated glitch."

"Liar," said Amelie coolly.

"Ready to go?"

"Absolutely!"

Amelie grabbed hold of the rope, Hugo sped away and Amelie showed the others what she'd learnt. She rose to her feet without a wobble, leant back and curved from side to side, spraying water and waving at them as if she really were the **irresistible** Julia Roberts.

"Now it's my turn," sighed Senta, as the second boat pulled up to the jetty.

She didn't make it to her feet, **toppled** into the water, resurfaced and swam back to the jetty. She made a second and a third **attempt**. "It's not my day today," she spluttered, clambering up the ladder to dry land.

It soon became **obvious** that Jannik and Nico were experienced water-skiers.

The longer Isa watched them, the less she felt like trying on the skis and **venturing** onto the water. But the others weren't having any of it.

---

expertly – meisterhaft; patronizingly – gönnerhaft; irresistible – unwiderstehlich; to topple – umfallen; attempt – Versuch; obvious – offensichtlich; to venture – sich vorwagen

"It's not as dangerous as it looks," Amelie reassured her. "You'll be just fine. All you have to do is stand up and balance, then it's **as easy as pie**."

"Easy-peasy," agreed Jannik, "that's all there is to it."

Isa obediently put on the skis, and promised to do exactly as Hugo told her. She didn't make it past the crouching position, of course, and landed in the water instead. The others yelled at her from the jetty: "Try again. You've got to try again."

And then, on her fourth attempt, it finally worked. She managed one whole lap, and came back brimming with **pride**.

"I knew you'd be a natural," said Nico, hugging her.

"Hey! What do you think you're doing?" protested Jannik, pushing him aside.

The others grinned.

After a while the instructors made it known that there were other people waiting to have a go.

"Who'll swim with me to the island?" shouted Amelie, who was bursting with energy.

No one felt like it apart from Nico.

"Isa, Jannik! You'll come, won't you? It's worth it, honest," said Amelie. "And it's not far either."

Isa, and then of course Jannik, let themselves be **persuaded**, and swam along too.

Amelie was right: it wasn't far. When they reached the shore, they hauled themselves out of the water over the pebbly beach and followed a narrow trail

---

as easy as pie – kinderleicht; pride – Stolz;
to persuade – überreden

leading steeply uphill. When they got to the top, the path zigzagged down the other side, back to the water.

"And now I'm going to show you the island's biggest secret," said Amelie, gesturing theatrically. "It's right here! This **cave** is a place for pirates and lovers. Nico and I found it when we were swimming here last week. We saw a few people sunning themselves on the rocks. So we swam over …"

"… and found the cave, just like that." Nico finished her sentence.

"That's great!" Isa was full of enthusiasm. The **hideout** in the rocks was the perfect place for her to jot down her thoughts in peace and quiet. If she wrapped her pen and paper in a plastic bag, they should be OK … And hadn't she promised Felix a letter? She'd write it in the cave, she decided.

Isa was pleased with the expedition, but was starting to feel cold. And she was hungry too. What was Florentine up to?

Luckily she wasn't the only one with **goose bumps** and an empty belly; the others wanted to get back as quickly as possible too.

"I'll come by for you on my way to dinner," said Jannik, through chattering teeth. "Agreed?"

Isa shook her head. "I'm going to dinner with Florentine. See you later, OK?"

---

cave – Höhle; hideout – Versteck; goose bumps – Gänsehaut

# Flotsam and Jetsam

Florentine wasn't in the bungalow.

Isa jumped under the shower, then pulled on her black jeans and her T-shirt with the pink and orange swirls, and tried to **tame** her hair.

The result was so **dispiriting** that she gave up entirely.

Florentine, she thought. Where's Florentine got to? It was time for dinner – her watch told her so, and so did her belly.

She must have gone on ahead, thought Isa. I bet she's sitting by the pool with Tersia, having fun. But didn't we say we'd do our own thing in the daytime and then meet up to eat? I'm sure that's what Florentine said …

Isa adjusted her hat and set off. She'd guessed right.

Florentine and Tersia were sitting contentedly by the pool.

"Aren't you hungry?" Isa called out to them from a distance.

They both laughed. "We're not in any hurry," said Florentine. "You can eat with your friends, if you like. We'll meet up later at the bungalow. Tersia and I have got lots to talk about – she's from the same town as we are …"

---

to tame – zähmen; dispiriting – deprimierend

"Really?" said Isa in astonishment, wondering how she'd managed to miss someone as **eye-catching** as Tersia, especially since she and her friends often hung out in town after school, watching people go past.

"I haven't lived there long," Tersia explained. "I've started a new job and I hardly know anyone. But I've had plenty of excitement already. My private life is a complete mess. I've got to start **sorting** it **out**."

Florentine looked at her questioningly.

Tersia wrapped one of her long blonde ringlets around her finger and narrowed her eyes. "Let's just say I've got a few different boyfriends, and now I'm supposed to settle on one. Can you believe it? I mean, it's not the kind of thing you can decide like that."

"What a difficult life you lead," laughed Florentine.

Isa was pleased with the way things were going. Florentine seems to be getting over her heartbreak, she thought, as she headed towards the dining hall. How lucky that she'd got to know Tersia!

The others were already sitting at "their" table.

"Where's Jannik?" asked Nico. "He's not with you, so what the hell have you done with him?"

Isa laughed. "Nothing. He's **bound to** come in a moment."

He didn't.

By the time they'd finished eating – which took quite a while – he still hadn't **materialized**.

"What do you think?" said Amelie. "Has he found another Isa?"

---

eye-catching – auffällig; to sort out sth – etw. in Ordnung bringen; to be bound to do – etw. tun müssen; to materialize – erscheinen

"Of course, he has," said Nico. "What else could he be up to? This is my chance."

He put his arm around Isa. "Forget Jannik: you've got me instead."

Isa shook him off. "What makes you think I want you? Or Jannik for that matter. I don't belong to anyone!"

"Ouch! No need to be so serious," Nico grumbled. "We're on holiday, we want to have fun – and it would be nice to have some happy memories for when we get home."

Isa looked at him.

"I'm on holiday, I want to have fun, but I don't want to be anybody's 'happy memory', got it?"

"Then I'll have to find someone less **prickly** than you," said Nico, pretending to be hurt. "Senta, would you like to be my 'happy memory'?"

"Why don't we go to the clubhouse?" said Senta, changing the subject.

Well, he's certainly not shy, thought Isa. "I came, I saw, I conquered" – what kind of an **attitude** is that!

It was only when Isa got back to Red Rose 31 at two o'clock in the morning that she **realized** Jannik was still missing.

I bet he's having problems with his dad, she thought. I wonder where he's staying. In the main hotel or in a bungalow? She really should have asked him ...

She yawned, unlocked the door, crept into the bathroom and reached for her toothbrush.

---

prickly – widerborstig; attitude – Haltung;
to realize – bewusst werden

Then she noticed that everything was still in its proper place – no traces of toothpaste around the sink, the tubes and jars lined up neatly, and nothing left lying around.

It's not like Florentine to go to bed with her make-up on, thought Isa, **unsettled**.

She put her toothbrush back into the glass and went to the bedroom. She left the bathroom door **ajar** so that she could see in the dark.

Florentine wasn't there. She wasn't in bed and she wasn't on the patio.

Isa turned on the lights and looked at her watch. Four minutes past two. Her tiredness was suddenly gone. She would have spotted Florentine, if she'd been in the clubhouse or by the pool, she was sure of that.

Maybe she was in Tersia's room?

The two of them were probably pouring out their sorrows, so busy complaining about men and about their own loser boyfriends that they'd forgotten the time. Or maybe they'd met some new people, were sitting out on a patio somewhere and sipping wine … No, thought Isa decisively. It's too cold to be outside. Unless … She looked in the wardrobe. Florentine's **emergency** jumper and her big thick **cardigan** were still there.

Isa took off her hat and **hurled** it onto the bed. Damn, she thought furiously. I don't know why I get so worried. She's twice my age – she should be taking care of me, not the other way round.

---

unsettled – besorgt; ajar – angelehnt; emergency – Not(fall); cardigan – Strickjacke; to hurl – werfen

She went out onto the patio. There was a dark-coloured object lying on the wall. It was Florentine's burgundy towel!

In the distance she heard voices. Women's voices. She could hear someone laughing, and then it sounded as if they were calling out. She stood on the wall and strained her ears.

She could definitely hear voices!

They were coming from across the water. It looked as though there was something out there.

A boat? Could it be a boat?

Suddenly she was sure she'd heard Florentine.

"Hello?" shouted Isa. "Hello there! Florentine? Is that you out there?"

She ran down to the beach. "Hellooo!"

Oh God, thought Isa. My **loopy** aunt is stuck in a boat with someone, and is drifting out to sea! What can I do?

She went back inside, saw her hat on the bed, pulled it over her head, and said to herself firmly: "This, Isa, is an emergency. What do you do in an emergency? You get help. But you don't know where Jannik lives, and you don't know where Tersia is either. So you'll have to go to reception and hope there's somebody there."

Isa left the lights on and **dashed off**.

She met two or three people wobbling home to bed, but no one who could be of any use.

Fortunately, there was a bell at reception. She pressed the buzzer and waited with baited breath.

---

loopy – irre;
to dash off – davonstürzen

After a few minutes Karen, the receptionist, appeared. She looked at Isa sleepily. "Yes?"

"My aunt's disappeared," gasped Isa. "You've got to help me find her! Please."

Karen yawned. She smiled at Isa friendly. "I expect your aunt would be horrified if we went looking for her now," she laughed.

"What do you mean?" asked Isa, puzzled.

Karen laughed again. "How old is your aunt? She must be over eighteen, huh?"

Isa nodded.

"OK … Is she here with her husband or her boyfriend? No? Well, I expect she's made a new friend and they're … they're … you know what I mean, huh?"

Isa shook her head. Then it **dawned** on her what Karen was trying to say.

"No," she said firmly. "My aunt's had enough of men. She just wants to be on her own right now."

"I can't believe it," groaned Karen. "How naïve can you get?"

"I'm not naïve. I'm worried," snapped Isa. "You have to help me, I'm serious. It's an emergency. She's stuck in a boat, drifting out to sea!"

Karen no longer looked so sure of herself. "Where did you get that idea from?"

"I heard voices out there. There was a dark shape on the water too."

"Which apartment are you in?"

"Red Rose 31," shot back Isa automatically.

"A bungalow on the seafront … OK."

---

to dawn – dämmern/einfallen

Karen thought for a moment, and then brightened up. "She can't be drifting away in a boat. The boats are brought in every evening and **chained up** on the shore. She can't have untied one. It's impossible."

Isa hesitated, thinking things over.

"If I were you, I'd forget about it. I'm sure nothing has happened to your aunt – or at least nothing bad … I expect she's back at the bungalow by now, lying in bed. She's probably worrying about you because you're not there. I bet she's wondering whether she should go and look for you. If we stand here any longer, she'll come running around the corner and demand a **search party** too!"

Isa laughed in spite of herself.

"You know what?" said Karen. "I think you should go straight back to Red Rose 31. I'm sure your aunt's in bed and imagining all the awful things that could have happened to you. Look, it's getting light already."

"But what if she's not there?" asked Isa.

"Then go to sleep and when you wake up, she'll be lying right next to you. Trust me, she'll be there."

Isa was **torn**. Karen's advice did sound reasonable. If she'd have been sharing a room with Amelie, for example, there'd only be one explanation if she failed to come home one night. But Florentine was different.

Florentine wasn't the kind of person to spend the night in someone else's bed. Especially after what had happened.

Or maybe precisely because of it?

---

chained up – angekettet; search party – Suchtrupp;
torn – [innerlich] zerrissen

Damn, thought Isa. If only she'd left me a note!

"I think I'll take a look ..." said Isa hesitantly. "But I might be back again later, OK?"

"OK," said Karen. "Sleep well and say hi to your aunt for me, won't you?"

Isa ran back.

The bungalow was exactly as she'd left it. The lights were on and there was no sign of Florentine. Isa stepped out onto the patio, walked down to the beach and scanned the sea and the **shore**.

Nothing. Although, **hang on**, what was that?

Isa held her breath. There was something in the water ... a boat? A boat.

She heard voices again. Isa laughed in relief. That was Florentine's voice, she was sure of it. But who was the other person? **Never mind** that: the main thing was she'd found Florentine!

She didn't bother shutting the doors, but sprinted back to reception and rang the bell, keeping her finger on the buzzer. "Hello? Hello? I've seen my aunt! It's an emergency!" She felt like an idiot, but what else could she do? Nothing!

"Oh, it's you again," said Karen **unenthusiastically**, pushing her hair out of her eyes.

"My aunt's in a boat with someone. I've seen them! Maybe they've lost the **rudder** or something, I don't know. In any case, they need help!"

Karen yawned and shook her head, trying to wake herself up. "Are you sure?"

---

shore – Küste; Hang on! – Warte mal!; never mind ... – ist doch egal ...; unenthusiastically – ohne jede Anteilnahme; rudder – Steuerruder

"One hundred percent … You have to help them!"

Karen reached for the telephone.

They waited for ages. No one answered.

She dialled another number. This time someone picked up.

"Hugo," said Karen, "I've got a problem. There's a girl here called …?"

"Isa!" said Isa. "And Florentine's my aunt."

"Isa's here and she's looking for her aunt. She says she's seen her in a boat."

"There's someone else there too," Isa interrupted.

Hugo said something and Karen laughed. "True. We've never had that before. It's got **novelty** value. Can you come round?"

She waited for him to answer, then put down the receiver.

"He's on his way," she said to Isa.

Hugo was there in no time. "I've seen you before," he said. "You were hanging out with the others on the jetty, weren't you? So, what's all the panic about?"

He listened **attentively**, but didn't seem particularly convinced. In the end, he agreed: "OK, let's take a look. But if you're right, I'd like to know how they got the boat afloat. We tie those boats up every night – they're absolutely **idiot-proof**."

Isa was right.

Florentine and Tersia were sitting onboard, and they greeted their rescuers with tears and smiles.

---

novelty – Neuheit; attentively – aufmerksam; idiot-proof – idiotensicher

"How did you manage to **untie** the boat?" demanded Hugo.

"Untie it?" echoed Tersia. Her teeth were chattering. "Thh... thh... there wasn't anything there to untie. Th... th... the boat was lying there – we just pushed it into the water."

"I'm not that **gullible**," said Hugo disbelievingly. "They're always tied up."

"B... b... but this one really wasn't," protested Florentine. "Only th... th... the rudder was m... m... missing. We th... th... thought we'd just bob up and down **in the shallows**. F... f... finish our b... b... bottle of wine and go to b... b... bed. B... b... but the stupid thing didn't stay in the shallows. S... s... suddenly we were right out to sea. Th... th... thank goodness you found us ..."

"And s... s... saved us," added Tersia fervently. "Lo... look here. Th... this is the bottle. If we'd had a c... c... cork and a piece of p... p... paper we could ha... have sent a message in a b... b... bottle!"

"Great. Well, that would have been a first." Hugo was annoyed with them. Even in the dark you could see and hear his **irritation**.

Florentine and Tersia were frozen. They were **shivering** and shaking **with cold**. They had to be lifted out of the boat onto the beach, and helped to their rooms.

"I'll take Tersia," said Hugo. "Can you deal with Florentine?"

"Course I can!"

---

to untie – losbinden; gullible – leichtgläubig;
in the shallows – im flachen Gewässer; irritation – Verärgerung;
to shiver with cold – frösteln

Isa fetched the woolly jumper from the wardrobe, pulled it over Florentine's head, helped her into bed, tucked her in, and put another layer on top.

Florentine's teeth were chattering.

"Do you have any brandy?" asked Hugo.

Isa shook her head.

"I'll see what I can do." He held on **tightly** to Tersia's arm. "Come on then!"

Isa sat down on the edge of Florentine's bed.

"So, how's our **shipwrecked** pirate?" she said. "What exactly were you looking for out there? Africa, maybe? No? I suppose that would have been a bit far, without water or **provisions**. No compass, no rudder, no sail – that would have been **daring**. And by the way, you forgot to leave me a note. It took me ages to work out where you were and to persuade anyone to help me."

"I'm really, really sorry," said Florentine through chattering teeth.

"Room service!" announced Hugo. He was carrying two hot-water bottles, a flask full of fruit tea and – a bottle of rum!

He sat down next to Florentine. "You'll soon be as warm as anything, just you wait and see. Open wide!" He made her **take a sip** of rum, then fruit tea, and then rum again. "Good girl," he praised her.

"You can take over now, Isa," he said after a while. "She'll have a stinking cold, but apart from that she'll be fine. I'll come back this evening, Florentine, and then you can tell me all about your midnight fishing.

---

tightly – fest; shipwrecked – schiffbrüchig; provisions – Vorräte; daring – kühn; to take a sip – einen kleinen Schluck nehmen

I rescued you, so I deserve to hear the story, it's only fair."

Florentine closed her eyes.

"Bye," said Hugo. "I'll be off now. Remember to put the 'do not disturb' sign up, Isa."

Suddenly she felt dead tired.

She locked the door to the patio, drew the curtains, pulled off her clothes and joined Florentine in bed. Wow, she thought, the rescue operation will fit perfectly with my article. A **genuine** real-life story … And then she fell asleep.

---

genuine – echt

# Emotional Rollercoaster

It was almost midday when Isa woke up. Her stomach was rumbling so **ferociously** that she got up straight away and got dressed. She wrote a note for Florentine: “Gone to lunch. Do not leave the room!!!”, and propped it up against the rum bottle.

To make doubly sure she took both keys with her.

“We’ve been waiting for you for ages,” said Senta **reproachfully**. “Did you come here to sleep or something? Jannik said the ‘do not disturb’ sign was hanging outside your door.”

Isa nodded. “And it’s still there. Hey Jannik, what happened to you last night? We were wondering where you’d got to.”

“I had to stay in. My dad was … He’d … He didn’t feel that well,” he explained weakly.

Everyone knew he wasn’t telling the truth.

“It happens to the best of us,” said Amelie quickly. “I expect he’s eaten something funny. Is he feeling better now?”

“Of course, he is; he’s **fighting fit**.”

“Well then … Isa, hurry up, will you? We’re going snorkelling with Hans. You’re coming too, huh?”

---

ferociously – wild; reproachfully – vorwurfsvoll;
fighting fit – topfit

Isa finished her mouthful. "I can't. I've got to look after my aunt."

"What?"

Before Isa could explain, Nico came up to the table. "Hi guys," he said excitedly. "Have you heard the latest? Hugo had to take to the seas last night to save a whole bunch of boatpeople."

"Really? Where were they from?"

"From here! Some idiots from the beach club managed to charter one of the boats and wanted to sail to India – or across the sea to Africa or whatever. Anyway, Hugo followed the **fugitives** in a motorboat and caught up with them just before they got to Turkey. It's really something! It's the first time anything like this has happened here. Everyone's really pleased – finally a bit of excitement **for a change**."

"Who told you about it?" asked Jannik.

"Hugo, I just saw him at the buffet. He …"

"Here he is," said Senta.

"So, how's your aunt? Everything OK?" He put his arm around Isa's shoulders.

Nico whistled through his teeth. He looked at Hugo, then Isa, then back at Hugo again. "Boatpeople … Does your aunt have something to do with this?" he asked.

Isa nodded.

"Well, go on then, tell all!" said Nico **impatiently**.

"What is there to tell? I've got no idea what she was up to. First of all she was too cold to talk, and then she fell asleep. She's probably still asleep now."

---

fugitive – Flüchtige(r); for a change – zur Abwechslung; impatiently – ungeduldig

"Was she on her own? Or did she bring a man and plenty of blankets?" asked Senta **eagerly**. "It's not a bad idea, if you think about it. Why don't you ever come up with things like that, Nico? Or haven't you **ticked** the box marked 'imagination'?"

"Just pass me a pen and I'll fill out the form," countered Nico, unruffled.

The others laughed. "So tell us then, Isa. Who was she with?"

"With Tersia and half a bottle of wine," said Isa. "I can just about laugh about it now, but I was really cross with her at the time. I was **worried sick**."

"I can understand that." Jannik looked deep into her eyes.

"I couldn't believe it at first," said Hugo. "It's the first time anything like this has happened. I'd like to know which careless idiot forgot to tie the boat up properly. I'll be having words with whoever it was."

"A boat trip by moonlight," said Senta. She rolled her eyes. "It sounds wonderful."

"Firstly, the moon is so thin that it's barely even visible at the moment. And secondly, it's so cold at night that absolutely nothing would happen. OK, so your nose might run, but I don't suppose that was what you had in mind," said Jannik.

"Wow! So you know all about it, do you? Did you untie the boat? Go on, **admit** it!"

"Nah, I've got nothing to do with the boat. It's just my dad was just sitting on the patio last night, count-

---

eagerly – eifrig; to tick – ein Kreuzchen machen;
worried sick – verrückt vor Sorge; to admit – zugeben

ing the stars. When I finally got him into bed he was as cold as frozen pizza. And he didn't even notice!"

"Has he got problems?" asked Amelie **compassionately**.

Jannik nodded.

"And your aunt? Does she have problems, or was she drunk?"

Isa shrugged. "Probably both. She's really annoyed with herself at the moment, and she's feeling a bit desperate. She wants to start again, but she doesn't seem to be able to …" She looked at Jannik.

"It takes time," he said knowledgeably.

"She needs a **distraction**," asserted Senta.

"Yeah, that's right. She should come snorkelling with us," suggested Nico.

Hugo shook his head. "I put sleeping-tablets in her tea. She won't wake up until the evening. But it's a great idea in principle. You should get her to join in and keep her busy, so she doesn't have time to think about things. Make sure she's got plenty to do, including stuff that she's good at. You can't do more than that."

"Oh yes, we can," said Senta. "We can **pair off** Jannik's dad with Isa's aunt. Then they can pool their sorrows and maybe they'll even like each other in the end. You never know."

"Bingo!" shouted Nico. "All old people play bingo! And afterwards they always say: 'It was the game that brought us together' … !"

"I'll try anything," said Isa, "but I'm not sure about bingo. Florentine isn't really the bingo type."

---

compassionately – voller Mitgefühl; distraction – Ablenkung; to pair off – verkuppeln

"My dad isn't either," said Jannik. "But we should **definitely** try everything else. And anyway, Isa, if your aunt isn't going to wake up until this evening, you can come snorkelling with us after all."

"No, you can't," said Hugo firmly. "The sleeping tablets weren't very strong, so I don't know when she'll wake up exactly. I think Isa should stay with her today. Sorry, honey."

"No problem." Isa wasn't **impressed**. She hadn't been able to sleep all night because of the excitement and now she was going to miss out on snorkelling too. And why? All because her aunt was on an emotional **rollercoaster**, courtesy of Bert-Wolfram.

"Looks like you've found a job," laughed Nico. "Aunt-sitting. See you later!"

When Isa got back to the bungalow, Florentine was fast asleep.

Isa touched her face. It was warm, but not hot. Reassured she gathered up her notepad, pens and nail-varnish collection and settled down on the patio in the sunshine. She rested the notepad on her knees, picked up her pen and paused. There was so much to write – where should she start? With Tersia? With the others? With water-skiing? With Florentine's watery adventure? With Hugo, when he ...

She **strained her ears**, and got up.

Florentine was awake.

"What time is it?" she asked.

"Just gone three ... Are you warm enough?"

---

definitely – auf jeden Fall; impressed – beeindruckt; rollercoaster – Achterbahn; to strain one's ears – die Ohren spitzen

"Y... y... yes!" sneezed Florentine. "Can you pass me a tissue, please? ... Atishoo!"

"That's exactly what Hugo said would happen," said Isa. "You've gone and got yourself a nasty cold."

Florentine stared at the ceiling. "Were you worried about me?"

"You can say that again! I didn't know where you were, and so when you didn't show up, I went to reception to get help. Karen was there, but she just laughed at me and said you'd be in bed with a **stranger**. I didn't believe her."

Florentine laughed.

"So what made you do it? It was freezing cold out there!"

"We weren't cold at all. I'd been at the bar with Tersia, and then she remembered she'd got some wine in her room. So we fetched the bottle and sat down on one of the boats on the beach. Tersia noticed it wasn't tethered up." Florentine blew her nose. "So we pushed it into the water. We couldn't find the rudder, but we only wanted to float around for a bit anyway. We were chatting and drinking, and then we saw you turn on the lights. It was only then that we noticed how far out we were ..." Florentine laughed again. "Just imagine: Tersia wanted to get out of the boat! But she couldn't touch the bottom and it was too cold to swim, so the only thing we could do was wait to be rescued."

"At least you weren't out at sea for too long," said Isa in relief.

"No, but it was long enough for me!" Florentine

---

stranger – Fremde(r)

dragged herself out of bed and headed for the bathroom. "I'm going to have a shower, and then I'll join you on the patio."

Isa nodded.

"How are you feeling?" she asked, when Florentine reappeared.

"Not so good. I still can't understand myself." Florentine sneezed several times in a row. "One thing is obvious: I'm not an **unfeeling** robot that plans everything and that thinks it's got a hold on its emotions and everyone else's too."

"Are there really people like that?" asked Isa **in astonishment**. "People who think they can control other people's emotions. That's crazy!"

"That's what you think," said Florentine. "I used to think so too, but some people really do believe that every little feeling and action can be planned."

"You're thinking of that guy again," said Isa. "You have to stop doing this."

Florentine shook her head. "I wish I could. But I still don't know what was going on in his head. You know – if two people love each other and then suddenly stop loving each other, it's just life. But it was different with us ..."

"What do you mean?" Isa was getting bored. She felt sorry for Florentine, but bad experiences were bad experiences. You just couldn't **avoid** them. She wanted to write to Felix. Felix! She sighed.

Florentine grinned. "Don't **pretend** you're interested ... You know, at first everything was fine. But

---

unfeeling – gefühllos; in astonishment – verblüfft;
to avoid – meiden; to pretend – so tun, als ob

then he started coming home later and later. Sometimes I couldn't get hold of him in the mornings. When I asked him about it, he always had an **explanation**. In the beginning I believed him – I mean, why shouldn't I have? But after a while I got **suspicious**. I told him there was only one explanation for his behaviour and that I wasn't a child any more. I'd had my own fair share of experience."

Isa nodded. "And then what happened?"

Florentine didn't care whether Isa was interested or not. She was determined to get it off her chest.

"And that's the next chapter of the story. He **denied** everything."

"That's really low."

"Yes, it completely confused me. When you love someone, you believe what they tell you. You should write that down too. Have you got a pen? Atishoooooo!"

"Have a tissue," said Isa. "And then what?" Isa wanted to hear the story after all.

"One day I came home, opened the door, and heard him saying on the phone: 'She's noticed things have changed, of course …' I asked him what he meant by that. He told me he'd been speaking to a **client**. What a creep!"

Florentine took another tissue from the packet. "I wanted to believe him, but everything I was seeing, hearing and noticing told me I shouldn't."

"It must be really horrible, not knowing where you stand," said Isa thoughtfully.

---

explanation – Erklärung; suspicious – misstrauisch; to deny – abstreiten; client – Kunde

Florentine nodded. "You can't put up with it for long. Although," she thought for a minute, "if you don't care about someone, you don't mind what they get up to."

"But if you like them ..."

"... things are very different." Florentine finished the sentence for her. "You know what, Isa? **I'm** absolutely **starving**. It's not time for supper yet, but we could get going anyway. Want to come? I'll just get changed."

They sat down by the pool. Florentine was sneezing and eating **crisps**. Isa was munching salted peanuts and watching the kids as they shot down the slide and splashed into the pool.

Hugo wandered past, caught sight of them and came over. "Everything all right now?"

Florentine nodded. "Thanks for the rescue operation and first aid." She sneezed.

Hugo raised his eyebrows. "And the boat really wasn't chained up?"

"Really and truly."

Hugo gave her a searching look. "I hope you and that other **nutcase** weren't trying to **hurt** yourselves."

"Rubbish," said Florentine emphatically.

"Good. But I still don't understand why the boat wasn't tied up. I don't suppose we'll ever know."

"Can I buy you a drink?" asked Florentine.

"Of course ..."

---

I'm starving! – Ich bin am Verhungern!; crisps – Chips; nutcase – Spinner; to hurt – verletzen

Isa grinned. Hugo shunted his chair across until he was sitting directly opposite Florentine.

"I'm glad you weren't hurt," he said and raised his glass.

Florentine, Isa and Hugo sipped their drinks and watched the people strolling around the pool. The doors to the mouth-watering buffet were still closed. Everyone stared fixedly at the ground – if they'd have looked up, the **glint** of **greed** in their eyes would have shocked the other passers-by.

Suddenly Isa noticed a man. His grasshopper-green checked trousers and his bright red nose made him easy to spot. He was **traipsing** around the pool, hands behind his back, brow furrowed, glancing hungrily towards the locked doors. But there was something odd about him ...

"Look over there," said Isa to Florentine. "That man's up to something."

He was – and they were about to see what.

A little girl **skipped** along in front of him. She had her hands in the air, arms clasped over her head, and was singing to herself and looking side-to-side. The man with the red nose clasped his arms over his head, moved his lips, and looked first this way and then that. He followed the little girl.

Everyone smiled.

A teenage boy with a tennis **racquet** under his arm walked up to a curly-haired girl who had just come out of an aerobics class. He smiled at her, talked to her, and put his hand on her arm. He was an utter

---

glint – Glitzern; greed – Essensgier; to traipse – latschen; to skip – hüpfen; racquet – Schläger

slime-ball. The man with the red nose stood three **paces** behind him and **copied** his every move.

The spectators laughed.

The slime-ball noticed. He turned around, saw the clown, lifted his racquet and was about to strike. The clown fearlessly copied him without **batting an eyelid**.

But before the tennis racquet could come crashing down, the red-nosed man found another victim. She was irresistible: tanned, leggy and just like something out of an advert.

She walked as though the pavement around the paddling pool were a catwalk on top of the world. She did it brilliantly, and the clown did it brilliantly too.

Everyone laughed – it was partly **admiration** and partly **spite**. But the girl wasn't just beautiful: she was funny and **gutsy** too. She whirled around, hugged the red-nosed man and gave him a kiss.

The spectators loved it. They clapped and called for an encore, but the clown took no notice. Shoulders hunched, hands behind his back, and frowning he carried on … until he found his next victim.

It was a man, not exactly young, but not old either. His trainers looked OK, as did his bermudas and his stripy polo-shirt with the requisite crocodile. All the same, he may as well have been carrying a sign saying "I'm a loser".

The clown slouched. His chest suddenly looked smaller, while his belly poked forwards. Instead of

---

pace – Schritt; to copy sth – etw. nachmachen;
to bat an eyelid – mit der Wimper zucken;
admiration – Bewunderung; spite – Bosheit; gutsy – mutig

gliding forwards he took small and careful steps – the very image of a middle-aged, middle-class conformist.

Until then Isa and Florentine had followed the clown's **transformation** with interest; but the sight of him looking so boring and bourgeois made them laugh out loud with the others.

Then he **moved** things **up a gear**. He'd just spotted someone whom he clearly found funnier; a man who looked as though he only needed to open his mouth and all these other unimportant people would get out of his way. He moved confidently, with a straight back, and arms swinging casually by his side. He **surveyed** the area watchfully – whenever a pretty girl walked past, he followed her with his eyes, staring **unashamedly**. He fished a **mobile** out of his pocket, looking every bit the successful workaholic on a short, sporty break.

The man with the red nose talked into his non-existent mobile, laughing, gesticulating, flirting with the handset and puffing up his chest.

"Hey!" Jannik suddenly appeared next to Isa.

"You're an unbelievably slow learner," hissed Isa. "I don't like people sneaking up on me. I've told you that before!"

"Leave him alone," said Florentine. "You shouldn't be so hard on him: he's not quite past the Red-Indian-phase yet. He's still playing 'brave Sioux and white squaw'."

---

transformation – Verwandlung; to move up a gear – einen Gang zulegen; to survey – betrachten; unashamedly – unverhohlen; mobile – Handy

"Rubbish!" Jannik let the **insult** wash over him. "We'd like to join you."

"Who's 'we'?" asked Florentine.

"Me and my dad."

"What? Is that your dad?" asked Isa in dismay. She pointed to the man with the mobile. "I imagined him completely differently."

"Well, go on then," said Florentine in amusement. "Bring him over here. With any luck he'll be just like you."

Jannik looked at Florentine **doubtfully**: was she making fun of him?

"Hello!" said Jannik's dad. "My name's Walter."

---

insult – Beleidigung; doubtfully – voller Zweifel

# The Mobile Man

Without waiting to be asked he drew up a chair, placed his designer mobile on the table and sat down. He took a quick look at Isa and Hugo; then he turned his full attention to Florentine. "Here on your own as well?" he asked **breezily**.

"No," replied Florentine with equal nonchalance. "You might be, but I'm certainly not."

Walter was taken aback.

Florentine laughed. "Surely my niece counts for something!"

"Oh, right ..."

Walter wasn't about to give up. "The kids are **in a different league**. I thought we could maybe ..."

"Kids, league ... The words are enough ..." said Florentine deliberately. She got up. "I'm hungry."

Walter jumped to his feet. "Me too. Let's go."

Hugo gave Florentine a nod. "Bye then ... Catch you later, OK?"

"Why don't you come too?" she said.

He shook his head and disappeared.

"Hello! Aren't you going to wait for us?"

Isa turned around. The whole group was on the move.

---

breezily – flott; to be in a different league – in einer anderen Liga spielen

"Did it work?" asked Nico, putting his arm around Isa's shoulders. "Have Jannik's dad and your aunt got any closer? Emotionally, I mean."

"They didn't really have a chance," said Isa regretfully. "Maybe we should all eat at the same table? What do you think?"

"No problem," Nico agreed **readily**. "Come on, people, there's plenty of room for us all."

Tersia waved at them from a distance. As usual, she put on a show for their benefit, but she did it so naturally and cheerily, with such obvious pleasure and good-humoured fun, that everyone just stared at her, enjoying the performance.

"Ladies, let's have one of you on either side – that would be perfect," said Walter breezily.

"Perfect for you maybe," said Tersia, "but not for us. Where would you like to sit, Florentine?"

Tersia and Florentine sat on the other side of the table. Tersia whispered something in Florentine's ear; then they both laughed and went to the buffet.

Jannik and Isa sat down next to each other.

"We're going **snorkelling** with Hans tomorrow. Do you and Florentine want to come too?" asked Jannik.

"I've never been snorkelling," said Isa, undecided.

Nico and Senta had been listening in. "Then you have to give it a go! We tried it this morning and we're going back tomorrow. Florentine …"

Florentine's seat was empty.

"She's gone to the buffet," said Isa.

Tersia returned, but there was no sign of Floren-

---

readily – bereitwillig; to snorkel – schnorcheln

tine. “She went back for some bread,” explained Tersia.

But she didn’t show up later either. After a while Isa started to **worry**. She decided to go looking for her.

Florentine wasn’t at the buffet, and she wasn’t at the bar. She hadn’t found another table, and she wasn’t by the pool. Florentine was gone.

“She’s bound to be in the bungalow,” Tersia reassured her. She nodded at Walter **graciously**, accepting his offer of a drink at the bar.

“The bungalow’s the only place she can be,” agreed Isa, and ran off. But her aunt wasn’t there either.

She walked back slowly towards the clubhouse. Nico, Amelie, Jannik and Senta were waiting for her there.

“What am I going to do? If I go with you guys to the disco, I won’t stop worrying the entire time,” said Isa helplessly.

Senta laughed. “It’s simple really. We’ll help you look. It’ll be fun, anyway.”

The others agreed. They set off.

First of all, they went to the beach. There was no one in the sea. While they were walking along the shore, they came across Hugo, who was busy checking all the boats and catamarans.

“No,” he said firmly. “There aren’t any boats missing today. Everything is fine. Is it something to do with Florentine? I can’t help you this time – I’m on duty this evening. Typical.”

---

to worry – sich Sorgen machen;
graciously – gnädig

"Maybe she's in the **gym**?" suggested Senta.

But the only person in the gym was a portly-looking man torturing himself on the rowing-machine. He glanced up at them and carried on.

Florentine wasn't in the TV room, the games room or by the fire.

They looked at each other helplessly. "I have to say, Isa, your aunt **has a** real **knack for** causing trouble," announced Nico.

"You don't say," said Isa. "Now there's only one place left to look. Have you seen the ancient ruins yet? No? Well, follow me."

By this time it was completely dark.

The moon was nowhere to be seen. The lights from the resort lit up only a small section of the beach, and no one had thought to bring a **torch** with them on holiday.

They set off undeterred.

After a while their eyes got used to the dark. They could now make out the dark outlines of the stones, rocks and trees, and in-between them some lighter shapes – the ruins and columns.

Giggling and laughing, they made their way along the waterline, shouting "Hello!" and "Florentine, where are you?".

Every now and then they stood still and listened. Nothing. "She can't have disappeared into thin air!" exclaimed Nico.

"Is that old cliché the best you can manage?" retorted Senta. But just as they were about to give up

---

gym – Fitnessstudio; to have a knack for sth – ein Händchen für etw. haben; torch – Taschenlampe and walk back, someone moved between two of the columns.

"Whoa, that's creepy!" whispered Senta, clinging on to Nico.

"Do you think I'm feeling comfortable?" he growled back.

"Florentine!" shouted Isa. "Florentine! It's us!"

For a moment the figure stood still; then it split into two bodies in a passionate **embrace**.

"Attention please!" yelled Nico. "Lights, camera, action!"

The couple moved apart, but soon fell back into each others' arms.

"It's not Florentine," said Isa. "She's got a completely different figure. And in any case, Florentine would have answered."

"Maybe she's been crying again and doesn't want us to see her?"

"Rubbish. It's too dark to see anything anyway," said Jannik.

"Besides, she wouldn't cry and then throw herself into someone else's arms," added Amelie.

They stood there, not sure what to do next.

"Look at the moon up there," said Senta. "It looks like something out of a **tacky advert**, huh?"

"Too right," agreed Nico. "It's utterly romantic – it seems a shame not to **seize** the moment."

He put his arm around Isa.

Isa pushed him away and Jannik coughed. "Who's going to kiss me then?" asked Senta.

---

embrace – Umarmung; tacky – billig/geschmacklos;
advert – Werbespot; to seize – ergreifen

They sat down on an overturned column and looked up at the moon. It was **suspended** in the sky in a narrow crescent. No one said anything.

The waves gently lapped the shore.

There were **rustling** sounds and birds flew noiselessly over their heads.

"**Bats**!" whispered Nico. "I bet they're bats! They must be."

"Ugh!" Senta jumped to her feet. "I'm not staying here any longer!"

"Calm down, will you. Bats aren't vampires. They won't hurt you," said Nico.

"Even so ... Are you guys coming?" pleaded Senta.

"There's no point in waiting here," said Isa. "Maybe Florentine's back in the clubhouse and having fun at the bar. There's going to be trouble, if I find her there!"

Despite the moonlight and the romantic atmosphere they walked back as fast as they could. They only slowed down when they reached the wide steps that led up from the beach to the pool. Isa was **anxious** but furious too.

"There she is!" said Senta suddenly. "That's her sitting over there."

"Florentine!" yelled Isa. "You can't just disappear like that. We were worried about you. We've been looking everywhere!"

"I don't need a babysitter, do I?" asked Florentine coolly.

"Err no," said Isa, taken aback. "Of course, you

---

suspended – frei schwebend; rustling – raschelnd;
bat – Fledermaus; anxious – besorgt

don't. But when you were floating away on the **tide**, you were pretty pleased to be rescued, weren't you?"

"You don't need to worry about me. I just got fed up earlier. Now I'm back again, I'm in one piece, and I'm perfectly happy. And I'm going to bed, OK?"

"To bed? Already?" Nico shook his head in disbelief. "You must be joking."

"There was one thing I wanted to ask you, Florentine," Jannik said quickly. "We're going snorkelling with Hans tomorrow morning. Do you want to come?"

"How early?"

"About ten o'clock. But if you're going to bed now, you'll have **plenty** of sleep."

Florentine thought for a moment. "Maybe. I'm not sure ... OK, I'll come along. Good night!"

They watched her go.

"Do you think she saw through our plan?" asked Isa. "She must have noticed something and then crept off because she isn't interested in Walter. Damn."

It was just after midnight when Isa unlocked the door to the bungalow. Florentine was lying in bed, reading.

"I thought you were supposed to be asleep," said Isa.

"It was a bit too early after all," replied Florentine, yawning loudly. "But now I'm really tired."

Isa undressed, washed, cleaned her teeth and slipped into bed. She'd been planning to ask Florentine why she'd disappeared from the dining-hall, but

---

tide – Flut; plenty – mehr als genug

as soon as she snuggled under the duvet, she fell straight to sleep.

At about half-nine the next morning Walter and Jannik came to pick them up. The others – Nico, Amelie, Senta and Tersia – were waiting on the beach. They were wearing **life jackets** over their swimwear.

Hans, their snorkelling instructor, was nearly two metres tall and very tanned. Tersia gave him her full attention.

He handed out the snorkels. "OK, guys, as you can see, there are two ends to a snorkel. You put one end in your mouth, like so …"

Tersia giggled.

"And, if you do it properly, the other end pokes out of the water and you can breathe. All right?"

"But what happens if my head goes in too deep?" asked Tersia innocently.

"Then the water will run in. It's obvious, isn't it? So make sure it doesn't happen."

"But what if it does happen?" persisted Tersia.

"Then you blow the water out again," Hans explained patiently.

"But," said Tersia, determined not to be put off, "what happens if I **inhale** the water?"

Nico lost his patience. "Then that's tough luck," he snapped.

A mobile went off. Walter fished the **gadget** out of his swim-bag, moved a few paces away, put one finger in his ear and said: "Yes … Yes … Speaking … OK, OK … Bye then!"

---

life jacket – Schwimmweste; to inhale – einatmen; gadget – Gerät

Tersia looked at him admiringly. "What a fascinating man you are, Walter. It's amazing how you do that."

"What's amazing about it?" asked Florentine irritated. "I can't stand those things – they're worse than the **plague** and the **taxman** put together."

"I have to be contactable at all times," said Walter meaningfully.

Nico coughed.

Jannik was drawing circles in the sand with his big toe.

"May we continue?" Hans was incredibly patient. "Good, so let's give it a go. Take a few strokes, put your head under water and breathe through the snorkel, got it?"

After a while Hans declared himself satisfied with their efforts. They clambered into the boat and the driver started the engine. Tersia found herself a seat where the breeze would be sure to blow her ringlets to maximum effect, while Walter squeezed in next to Florentine, who promptly slid to the other end of the bench.

Jannik was staring determinedly at the **spray**. Isa felt sorry for him.

"Don't **get** so **worked up** about your dad," she said to him softly. "It's not your fault he's so **full of himself**. There's nothing you can do about it."

"He used to be so different," said Jannik quietly. "I used to think he was fairly normal – whereas now!

---

plague – Pest; taxman – Finanzbeamte(r); spray – Gischt; to get worked up – sich aufregen; to be full of oneself – eingebildet sein

Now he's so revolting no one wants to be around him any more. It's horrible. And frustrating too."

"It'll pass," said Isa hopefully. "You wouldn't believe how much my aunt has changed. She used to be so funny. She used to have so much energy she could **barely** sit down for more than two seconds – she made James Bond look boring. And now? Now she goes to bed at nine! Does that make sense to you?"

They sat in silence.

"Look at them," said Jannik. "From the outside they look fine, right? But on the inside they're all **messed up**. You know what? I like your hair, I like your wacky fingernails, I like the way you laugh – you're exactly my type, I reckon. But that's as far as it goes. After that I put my foot on the **brakes** and pull down the hatches. The last thing I need is that kind of drama. I want to stay cool, that's all. Know what I mean?"

Isa nodded. "I can see how you might feel that way. I read something recently: 'Don't flirt with disaster.'"

Jannik laughed. "Don't flirt with disaster. Exactly," he echoed.

Isa frowned. "But I still don't really get it. If that's your attitude, why did you keep **pestering** me? That wasn't very cool. Go on, explain that to me!"

"What's there to explain?" asked Jannik in surprise. "I told you, I like you. That's enough, isn't it?"

"God, you're complicated! Back home I've got a boyfriend. He's called Felix, and he'd never dream of **stopping short** just so as not to **be disappointed**."

---

barely – kaum; messed up – verkorkst; brake – Bremse; to pester – belästigen; to stop sth short – etw. abbrechen; to be disappointed – enttäuscht werden

"Well, he hasn't had to put up with my dad and my experience. He must be one of the lucky ones."

Isa thought for a moment. "True," she said.

Jannik screwed up his eyes. "And you?" he asked softly. "Which group do you belong to?"

"How do you mean?"

"How are things for you at home?"

"Fine," said Isa, embarrassed. "Everything's fine. Sometimes my parents go on at me for spending too much time on other stuff and not on my schoolwork, but **apart from** that they leave me and my brother in peace."

"And what's up with Florentine?"

"I'm not sure," said Isa. "Something went badly wrong with her ex-boyfriend. She keeps **hinting** at what happened, but she hasn't really said. She's not ready to talk about it yet."

Jannik didn't say anything.

The motorboat was chugging towards a little island. It gradually slowed down until it came to a halt and Hans let down the **anchor**.

He checked everyone's life jackets were on properly and then made them show him how to breathe through their snorkels. Then he packed them off into the water.

At first Isa just circled the boat and took care to breathe exactly as Hans had told her. But she soon gained confidence, and ventured further away. She looked at the underwater rocks, niches, caves and coves in fascination. The fish were small and brown,

---

apart from sth/sb – von etw./jmd. abgesehen; to hint – andeuten; anchor – Anker

but she still couldn't stop watching them – everything underwater looked so strange and different.

She waited until she was completely frozen before she swam back to the boat. She **hauled** herself slowly up the ladder. She was the last one back.

The others were warming themselves in the sun and eating segments of orange that Hans had laid out on a round tray. They drank juice and swapped stories.

"We saw a **moray eel**, didn't we Senta?" said Nico. "They're really dangerous."

"Did it **take a nibble**?" Only Tersia could ask something like that. "I was pricked by a **sea urchin**."

Hans laughed. "You wouldn't be looking so cheerful, if that were true. Do you know what sea urchins look like?"

Everyone nodded.

"Good. Well, be careful not to **tread** on one. We've got thirty minutes until we have to head back. You can have another snorkel, if you like."

Florentine was standing at the railings, undecided.

"Shall we take another dip, Florentine?" asked Walter.

Florentine raised her eyebrows. "We? Which 'we' would that be?"

"You and me, Florentine."

Florentine glanced over at Tersia, who was letting herself be strapped into her life jacket by Hans. "I'm not in a fit state to be part of a 'we' at the moment, Walter. You should **keep** your **distance**."

---

to haul – ziehen; moray eel – Muräne;
take a nibble – ein Stück abbeißen; sea urchin – Seeigel;
to tread – treten; to keep distance – Abstand halten

His mobile rang.

"... taking care of your mobile and not of me. Are you coming, Isa?"

"I haven't warmed up yet," said Isa. "Maybe later."

Florentine nodded and sprang into the water.

Isa watched her. She was a good swimmer, and she swam with long, even strokes. You could tell from watching her that she was sporty and well-toned.

She dived, came up again, blew the water out of her snorkel, and dived back under. This time she went deeper and stayed down longer – she seemed to be having fun. She swam towards a rock, and then suddenly, without warning, jerked back, **flailed** her arms, came up to the surface and disappeared underwater. In no time Hans was in the water. He swam frantically towards her until he was alongside her. In one quick **movement** he turned Florentine onto her back, put his arm under her chin and swam with her towards the boat.

Nico, Jannik and Walter were waiting at the top of the ladder. They grabbed Florentine, pulling and heaving her over the side of the boat and onto the floor.

She gasped for air.

Hans knelt down, pulled her towards him, and lifted her arms up and down above her head until she stopped **wheezing**. She started taking in short, quick gasps of air until she was finally breathing regularly again.

"You poor thing," said Tersia. She wiped the

---

to flail – herumfuchteln; movement – Bewegung;
to wheeze – keuchen

droplets from Florentine's face, stroked her hair, knelt down and held her hand.

Isa suddenly realized that she was clutching onto Jannik's arm. "Whoops, sorry."

Jannik grinned. "That was a bit of a shock, huh?"

Walter was standing next to Hans, fiddling with his mobile. "I was about to call for an ambulance. You see how useful mobiles can be."

No one said anything.

"Are you all right now?" asked Hans cautiously.

Florentine nodded.

Isa sat down on the other side of her. "What went wrong?"

"I don't know." Florentine's voice sounded **hoarse**. She cleared her throat. "I **swallowed** some water, couldn't breathe properly and then panicked. I'm really sorry."

"No need to be." Hans turned to the man at the wheel. "We should go back now. Have we got everyone?"

He helped Florentine to her feet, and guided her to the bench.

---

hoarse – heiser; to swallow – schlucken

# A Colourful Burger

After lunch Florentine and Isa relaxed on the patio in the sun. Florentine **dozed off**, while Isa sat, notebook on her knees and pen in hand, trying to bring some order into her impressions of that morning, so that she could start to put them down on paper.

She wasn't having much luck: there was so much to write about she didn't know where to start. Take Tersia and her magnificent ringlets; she always looked as if she had just emerged from a salon. Relaxed and **self-assured**, she'd flirt with any **available** man. She was just the kind of woman everyone loves to hate, but she was cheery and energetic too.

Isa thought of Walter and how he got on everyone's nerves with his mobile. He treated it like a weapon: don't you dare come too close, I'm a very important person – **there's** so much **more** to me **than meets the eye** … And then there was Jannik, who couldn't **come to terms with** the way his dad had changed. He was so afraid of having to deal with more problems that he wouldn't open up to anyone or anything and was well on his way to becoming a **toad**.

---

to doze off – eindösen; self-assured – selbstbewusst; available – verfügbar; There's more than meets the eye. – Da steckt mehr dahinter.; to come to terms with sth – sich mit etw. abfinden; toad – Miststück

Senta, Amelie and Nico were the only ones really enjoying themselves, thought Isa.

At that point she decided to stick with describing her experience of snorkelling and to only write about what she'd seen underwater.

In bold, flowing letters she wrote down her heading: "Snorkelling".

"When you go snorkelling," she wrote, "you dive underwater. You dive down and enter another world. Everything is quiet. You can only hear the sound of your own breath. You can't talk; you can only communicate with other snorkelers through gestures. That changes everything. Whenever you feel like saying something – even if it's just to tell someone that there's a **shoal** of fish swimming their way – you can't. When you're underwater, you have to use **sign-language**. It's not the place to talk or listen. I think ..."

"Hello!"

Isa jumped. "Do you always have to creep up on me like that?" She glared at Walter and Jannik, who had just appeared on the patio from the beach. "It really **bugs** me!" she said angrily.

"Sorry," said Jannik ruefully. "I thought you'd seen us coming. You kept looking in our direction."

"I wasn't watching you: I was writing and concentrating on my thoughts!"

"OK, OK," said Florentine soothingly. "What are you two up to?"

"First of all, we wanted to check you're OK," replied Walter, "and then we were planning to swim

---

shoal – Schwarm; sign-language – Zeichensprache;
to bug sb – jmd. auf die Nerven gehen

out to the island. We wondered whether you'd like to join us. Nothing can happen to you there, Florentine."

"I'm fine now," laughed Florentine. "And I'd love to swim out to the island with you, but only if you leave your mobile behind and promise that it's just the swimming you're after."

"That won't be too easy for me," said Walter. "But I'll do my best, for your sake, Florentine."

"Are you coming too, Isa?" asked Jannik.

Isa nodded. "You've made me lose my **train of thought** now anyway."

"Is that a love letter you're writing?" he demanded.

"What do you think!" shot back Isa.

Jannik and Walter were strong swimmers, just like Isa and Florentine. They soon reached the island, but because that side of it was covered in stones and sharp rocks, they decided to swim around a bit further until they got to the little sandy bay.

"I **bet** the whole of the beach club will be lying there, roasting in the sun," said Florentine.

She was wrong. To her surprise they were the only ones there. They chose the nicest, sandiest, warmest bit of beach and stretched out there.

"I'm bored," said Jannik after a few minutes. "I'm going to explore the island, even if it **tears** my feet to pieces. Feeling brave, Isa?"

"Brave enough. I'm coming too."

---

train of thought – Gedankengang;
to bet – wetten; to tear – reißen

Jannik surveyed the area. "If we take this route over the rocks, we'll be halfway up already." He set off. The first section was easy: the sea had smoothed the sloping stone slabs, and they were pleasantly warm. After that came prickly undergrowth, which they tried their best to avoid. They soon found a **groove** in the rock that had been hollowed out by the rain, and got to the top relatively unscathed. There they had a fantastic view of the mainland and the resort.

"Look! There's the jetty!" called out Isa in excitement, laughing at the water-skiers, as they wobbled and splashed into the water.

The catamarans were sailing in the bay, leaving white trails of spray behind them. A few canoeists were paddling near the shore. They saw people on the poolside, kids playing in the paddling pool and on the slide, and a group of older children trying to build a **tee-pee**, while another set played beach ball.

"It's really nice here," said Isa, "don't you think, Jannik?"

"Hmm? Yeah, nice," he said uncommunicatively.

"What's wrong with you?" asked Isa. "You could at least show a bit of enthusiasm!"

"What for? Just to please you? I don't think so."

Isa looked at him thoughtfully. "You're so ... I don't know how to describe it. To start with, you're so **detached**: you act as if nothing could surprise you. And you won't let anything affect you – you're not even pleased to be here, to have this incredible view or whatever ... Why are you so **repressed**?"

---

groove – Rille; tee-pee – Tipi; detached – distanziert; repressed – verklemmt

"I'm not repressed!" protested Jannik. "I just want to be left in peace!"

"OK," said Isa. "So why didn't you swim out to the island on your own then? Why did you come snorkelling this morning? Why do you keep calling for me? Why do you want me around?"

"Why, why, why? Why do you ask so many questions?"

"Because I don't understand you," replied Isa. "You can't eat a Big Mac with your mouth closed, but that's exactly what you're trying to do."

"Come again? I'm not following."

"It's simple really," said Isa. "You'll only ever be left in peace if you're alone. If you're with someone else, like me for example, then I'll say something to you, ask you something, show you something, and before you know it, your **peace and quiet** has vanished. And why's that? Because we're not silent creatures, that's why. And when I ask questions, I usually expect an answer."

"That doesn't mean to say I have to give you one. I don't have to do anything I don't want to."

"True, but don't go looking for company then. If you hang out with other people, you have to get involved."

"That's too stressful."

"And it's stress you want to avoid, huh?"

"Yeah, I mean, who needs stress? But I still like having you around. I can't stand being on my own."

Isa looked at him **in despair**. "But you can't just

---

peace and quiet – Ruhe und Frieden;
in despair – verzweifelt

help yourself to whichever bit of me you happen to fancy – you have to take the whole package!"

"Maybe with you I do, but not with everyone else," said Jannik **pigheadedly**.

"OK, I wasn't talking about everyone else: I was talking about me. I don't want to be the sesame seed or tomato on your Big Mac, all right? If you only want sesame seeds or a slice of tomato, you'll have to find someone who only wants some sesame seeds or tomato in return!"

"Why are you so **wound up** about it?"

"Because you won't see that you're asking the impossible: you want to hang out with me, but you want me to leave you alone. How's that supposed to work?" Isa glared at him. "And anyway, I'm supposed to be here to enjoy myself."

She looked at the amazing view: the blue sea, the silvery glint of the waves, and the even deeper blue of the sky. She felt the warmth of the sun on her skin and the earth under her feet and thought of the person standing next to her, who couldn't share in her amazement, excitement and pleasure.

So maybe there were people who liked to carry their feelings around in heavily **armoured** boxes; but that didn't mean she had to hang out with them. She shook her head and looked around for Jannik. He was standing there with **hunched** shoulders and such a miserable face that she couldn't help laughing.

"Come on then!" she shouted boisterously. "You wouldn't be able to cope with a whole Big Mac any-

---

pigheadedly – starrköpfig; to be wound up – sich aufregen; armoured – gepanzert; hunched – gekrümmt way – your little teeth are afraid of **crunchy** edges! They only go for the nice soft **titbits**!"

Isa laughed all the way down the hill to where Florentine and Walter were waiting. Jannik and his love of titbits! They scrambled and slid down the rocks. They'd almost got down to the sea when Isa **stumbled,** caught herself, turned around – and saw the pirates' cave.

"Want to take a look?" she asked Jannik. Florentine's voice rang out.

"Is that you? We were beginning to think you'd vanished. If Walter hadn't left his mobile behind, he'd have called the mountain rescue!"

"There's a cave over here!" shouted Isa. "Do you want to come and see?"

Jannik stood at the opening and looked into the darkness. "How far back do you think it goes?" he asked.

"How should I know?" Isa pushed him to one side and went in. After only a few paces she said in disappointment: "It's not a **proper** cave at all. It's just a little **niche**. Look, it doesn't go any further. What a shame!"

"Let me see – maybe you haven't looked properly," said Florentine. "I think there's a chink in the rock over here ... Oh, only a mouse would be able to **squeeze through** that."

"Let's swim back!" said Isa. If they went now, there'd still be enough time before dinner for her to

---

crunchy – knusprig; titbit – Häppchen; to stumble – stolpern; proper – richtig; niche – Nische;
to squeeze through sth – sich durch etw. durchzwängen

finish writing, wash her hair and paint her nails. She was going to use a bright red nail varnish – vivid red with silver diagonal zigzags. That would fit her mood perfectly!

Florentine screamed. "Ouch! Ow!" She was clutching one of her feet with both hands. "That really hurt!"

"Florentine, what have you done now!" exclaimed Isa. "You must be the **unluckiest** person alive!"

Florentine was sitting on a rock, holding her right foot and fighting back the tears.

"Did you **stub your toe** or something?" asked Jannik.

"Here, let me take a look!" Walter was there in no time. All three of them bent down to **examine** Florentine's foot. You could see little black dots on her sole near the heel. There were specks of blood, plus a few thin splinters sticking out of the flesh.

"Do you know what you've gone and done?" asked Walter. "Exactly what Hans told us not to: you've trodden on a sea urchin."

"Congratulations," said Jannik.

"What am I supposed to do now?" Florentine was still trying not to cry. "How am I going to get these things out of my skin? Go on, tell me that, if you're so clever!"

"The **spines** have to be taken out with **tweezers**," said Walter. "But I haven't got any with me."

"And you haven't got your mobile either!" Florentine had recovered sufficiently to tease him.

---

unlucky – glücklos; to stub one's toes – sich die Zehen anstoßen; to examine – untersuchen; spines – Stacheln; tweezers – Pinzette

"There's a **first aid** place in the hotel," said Jannik. "I've seen it: it's right next to reception."

They pulled out the spines that were poking out the furthest, and helped Florentine, who could only use one foot, into the sea. They swam back and headed towards the first-aid room.

A young doctor examined Florentine's foot. "It's nothing serious. It's always happening here. I'll do my best to remove the spines, but lots of them have already broken off, so I won't be able to get them all out. The rest will work their way to the **surface** in due course."

"We'll see you later," said Walter hastily, disappearing with Jannik.

Isa held Florentine's hand while the doctor got to work. It was a painful business. He pushed, pinched and **tweaked** until he finally declared that he could do no more. He disinfected Florentine's heel and wrapped it in a magnificent bandage.

"Will you be able to walk like that?"

Florentine nodded. "I'll just have to put my weight on my toes."

"Give me a call if it really starts to hurt, though I don't expect it will. I imagine it will burn and **twinge** for a while, but in two to three hours the worst should be over. By dinner time you'll be fine."

"Let's hope so," said Isa, setting off with Florentine.

Their progress was slow, even though Florentine was hobbling as best she could.

---

first aid – erste Hilfe; surface – Oberfläche; to tweak – zupfen; to twinge – stechen

Florentine **cursed** softly as they walked past the pool and down the stairs onto the path, but when Isa started laughing, she couldn't help joining in. Soon the two of them were in hysterics.

"Florentine! I can't believe it! What have you been up to this time?" They heard footsteps behind them, and saw Hugo hurrying towards them, staring at them in disbelief. "I thought you'd used up all your bad luck this morning – Hans was telling me that you were trying to **beat** the fish."

"What?" queried Florentine. "Trying to beat the fish? How do you mean?" She wiped away her tears of laughter and nearly fell over.

Hugo propped her up again. "I'll tell you in a minute. Come on, you'll be fine if you take it slowly."

"So what was that about fish?"

"You must have slept through your biology lessons. Don't you know fish take in oxygen by pumping water through their **gills**?"

Isa laughed, but Florentine looked at him blankly.

"It's obvious really," explained Hugo. "You thought you could get by on the oxygen in the water. But you haven't got gills, so you couldn't filter the oxygen and it all went horribly wrong." He stopped joking. "You were really lucky this time, Florentine, you know that, don't you?"

Florentine nodded.

"So, tell me what happened to your foot."

Florentine grimaced. "Two words: *sea … urchin.*"

"Sh… That's **lousy**. Where did you find it?"

---

to curse – fluchen; to beat sb – jmd. Konkurrenz machen; gill – Kieme; lousy – beschissen

"On the island."

"Well, that's not surprising. You should never walk barefoot on the island, didn't anyone tell you?"

"Like whom exactly?" asked Florentine. "It's not that bad really. The worst thing is that there were four of us out there – Walter, Jannik, Isa and me – but I was the one who had to go and get her poor delicate foot all covered in spines."

Hugo stood still. "Florentine." His expression was serious. "Florentine, I can only **advise** you to stay in your room, lie in bed, have your meals delivered. Don't put a foot outside until it's time to go. You **attract** bad luck like ..."

"... like iron is attracted to the North Pole?" suggested Isa.

"Exactly. Like iron is attracted to the North Pole," echoed Hugo. "So here we are: Red Rose 31. Will you manage on your own?"

"No problem." Isa unlocked the door.

"And Florentine, stick to my advice. If I had my way, I'd lock you in a tower like Rapunzel – then you'd really be safe."

Florentine stopped, turned around and looked at Hugo thoughtfully. "Tell me, Hugo, dearest, why is it you're so worried about me?"

She raised her eyebrows provocatively, and waited for him to reply.

Hugo stuffed his hands deep into the pockets of his baggy Bermudas. "I'm not worried about you, Florentine. I'm worried about the club. Your endless accidents aren't good for our image!"

---

to advise – beraten; to attract – anziehen

Florentine **blushed**. "I see ..." she said slowly.

"Well, what were you thinking?" He grinned and walked away. After a few paces he turned around and shouted: "I'll have your meals delivered to you!"

"**Don't bother**!" yelled Florentine. "I'll only send them back!"

---

to blush – rot werden; Don't bother! – Lass nur!

# The Titbit System

Florentine stretched out in the deck-chair, put her feet up, folded her arms behind her head and closed her eyes.

"What rubbish! As if you could be bad for anyone's image!" Isa was **outraged**. "You're still coming to dinner with me, aren't you?"

"Of course, I am!" said Florentine firmly. "I'll just wait until the pain has died down a bit and then I'll get changed."

"Good. I'll get showered," said Isa, and disappeared.

After a while she came back carrying her nail varnish collection and sat down on the wall at the edge of the patio. She painted busily.

"What are you laughing about?" asked Florentine sleepily.

"Me? Laughing? I was just thinking about Jannik. He's enough to make you want to run away."

"I thought you two were getting on fine."

Isa shook her head. "He's nice enough – so long as you don't get to know him too well. And if you do – my God!"

"That sounds **intriguing**. Go on then, what's wrong with him?"

---

outraged – empört; intriguing – faszinierend

Isa thought for a moment. “Imagine a burger. If you start with the bottom, you’ve got half a burger-bun, a **lettuce-leaf**, a squashed bit of meat, a slice of tomato, some gherkin, onion rings, mayonnaise and then the other half of the bun. Got it?”

Florentine nodded.

“And now imagine that this big fat **juicy** burger is lying on a plate in front of you, and you’re hungry. What would you do?”

“Silly question. I’d eat the big fat juicy burger.”

“How?”

“How would I eat it? With my fingers of course! Or do you think I should fetch some cutlery? Maybe I could set the table with Great-Aunt Gertrude’s white damask tablecloth too!”

Isa giggled. “I didn’t mean it like that. I meant, how would you eat the burger? In whole bites or **layer** by layer?”

Florentine sat up straight. “Isa, have you been out in the sun too long? Maybe you’ve got **sunstroke**?”

“Of course, I haven’t. I’m fine! So, tell me, how would you eat the burger?”

“I’d take one bite after the other. How about you?”

“The same.”

Florentine lay back again. “So what’s the burger got to do with Jannik, if you don’t mind me asking? Is there a point to this?”

“Don’t be so impatient: I’m getting there,” said Isa, and described the conversation she’d had with Jannik on the island.

---

lettuce-leaf – Salatblatt; juicy – saftig; layer – Schicht; sunstroke – Sonnenstich

"You know what, Florentine," concluded Isa, "at school the teachers only see bits of you as well. When you're good at a subject, you're like the crunchy lettuce leaf. If you're not up to much, you're the mushy tomato. That's just how it is. It's only at home, when you're with your family, that you're all these different things at once. Then you're ... you're ..." Isa was trying to find the right word.

"**The whole works**?" suggested Florentine.

"Exactly! My parents don't see me as being good in one place, bad in another and **average** somewhere else. For mum, dad and my brother I'm just 'Isa'. Felix sees it the same way as I do. OK, so we've never actually talked about it, but it's obvious that he does. But Jannik is completely different. Jannik is nice enough, so long as you leave him in peace. As soon as you get too close to him, he tries to block you out. Do you see what I mean?"

Florentine nodded.

"I see exactly what you mean, Isa. But suppose you fell in love with Jannik, and because you were so **besotted** with him, you didn't notice that the only bits of you he was interested in were the lettuce-leaf, the gherkin and maybe the tomato?"

"But what about the meat and the mayonnaise?" asked Isa.

"He'd get them from a different burger."

"You mean he'd take two burgers and make a third?"

"Well, yes, if you take lots of different parts, you can still get a whole."

---

the whole works – das Gesamtwerk; average – durchschnittlich; besotted – völlig vernarrt

"And what would he do with the **leftover** bits?"

"He'd throw them away. He doesn't need them, so they're not important to him. In fact, he finds them **inconvenient**. At first he pushes them to the side of his plate, but they keep sliding back into the middle."

"And then he gets the feeling he has to get rid of them."

Florentine laughed. "And that's precisely the problem. You can easily throw away a mushy piece of gherkin, but people aren't burgers: you can't take one titbit from here and another from there without them protesting."

Isa frowned.

"It's hard to imagine it," she said. "It's much better to have one big fat juicy burger, without taking it apart!"

"Some people find that boring. They prefer to mix things up a bit. Besides, it gives them the opportunity to take a bite out of several burgers. And that gives them the illusion of having **greater choice** – and choice for them means freedom."

"I guess it's possible," said Isa thoughtfully.

"What's possible?" Tersia jumped over the little wall. "I hear you've been fighting with a sea urchin, Florentine. Your foot's all bandaged up, you poor thing!"

"It's not that bad," said Florentine. She signalled to Isa that they'd carry on their conversation another time. She got up. "I'll be ready in a second, and then we can go to dinner, OK?"

---

leftover – übrig geblieben; inconvenient – lästig;
greater choice – mehr Auswahl

The next morning Florentine decided to have a day of rest.

She pushed her deckchair into the sunshine, placed some books, magazines and fruit within reaching distance, and made herself comfortable.

Isa promised to come back at one and pick her up for lunch. She pulled a T-shirt on over her bikini, gave her aunt a hasty kiss and ran down to the beach to meet the others at the jetty.

"Doesn't look so good today," said Nico. "I don't know where all these people have come from."

Senta, Amelie and Jannik **budged up** to make room for Isa. She squeezed in between them and glanced around. "Ugh! All these **past-it** people ... Why don't they just go and sunbathe on the beach?"

"Exactly. Let the young people enjoy themselves, that's what I say," agreed Nico.

To their astonishment the middle-aged folk proved extremely **proficient** on water-skis. They were so good that Hugo and the other **instructors** took them further and further out to sea. You could tell they were enjoying themselves too.

After they'd waited for ages and had only been out once, Jannik said: "I give up. How about a game of tennis instead?"

"Too much **effort**," said Senta, and the others agreed.

"Beach ball then?"

"No way!"

"Aerobics?"

---

to budge up – zusammenrücken; past-it – zu alt; proficient – fähig; instructor – Lehrer; effort – Mühe

"Yuck!"

"I know!" Senta jumped up. "The catamarans! We haven't tried them yet."

They talked it over and decided to go and have a look before **making up** their **minds**. "After all, we're not like our parents – we don't have to keep **proving** ourselves. There's no need to prove anything when it's obvious we can do it!"

"Yeah, we're supposed to be on holiday."

Jo, a small and wiry-looking man, was teaching a handful of eager **novices** how to sail a catamaran.

"Isn't that your dad?" asked Senta, pointing to a man in a pair of bright green trunks.

"Oh God, I'm out of here!" said Jannik in horror, hiding behind his sunglasses.

"Don't be ridiculous! Let's sit on the beach and watch," said Senta firmly.

Jo dashed from one side of the boat to the other, explaining how to raise the **sails** and keep them up. Then he asked for a volunteer to put the theory into practice.

Jannik's dad came forward.

"Nicely done," the others **praised** him.

Jo showed them how the rudder works.

Jannik's father demonstrated.

The others clapped enthusiastically.

And so it went on: Jo showed them what to do, and Walter demonstrated. The pattern had been established, and no one else could get a look in.

---

to make up one's mind – sich entscheiden;
to prove oneself – sich beweisen; novice – Anfänger; sail – Segel; to praise – loben

"His mobile," said Isa suddenly. "No one's rung his mobile since we got here. It must be awful for him, Jannik."

"He'll say it wasn't **switched on**," said Senta. Everyone laughed.

In the end, Jo asked the group if they now knew how to sail a catamaran.

"No problem," his pupils chorused nervously.

Senta giggled. "I bet they end up in the water."

Jo seemed satisfied. "Just go for it!" he shouted cheerfully. "Now get into pairs and push the catamarans into the water."

In twos they found a catamaran, pushed it into the water and leapt onboard.

Walter was only half a pair. He glanced around and spotted Jannik, but before he could call his son, Jo clapped his hand on his shoulder and said brightly: "Come on, Walter, you're my second!"

"Phew!" Jannik pretended to wipe the sweat from his forehead.

The others laughed. "That was a lucky escape!"

Jo, of course, was an absolute expert. Nothing could go wrong with him onboard.

"Push the rudder to the right!" he yelled across the water to one of the pairs. "To the right, I said. To the right! No, the right!" The couple were pushing the rudder as hard as they could to the left. The sails were fluttering and the boat was leaning dangerously to one side.

Jo shot over towards them in his catamaran and turned at the last minute: "Look, this is how you

---

to switch on – einschalten

have to do it! Or do you want to **capsize**?" At long last, the couple **grasped** the difference between left and right. It was lucky they did because another boat was heading towards a group of surfers, sails billowing and full speed ahead. The surfers wobbled on their boards and struggled with the wind, waves and **gravity**. They certainly weren't in a position to dodge a catamaran.

Jo managed to head the boat off in the nick of time, saving the surfers and the catamaran.

"Blimey! I'd hate to have his job!" said Isa. "They're absolutely out of control. They make my aunt look great!"

"My dad's not doing too badly," said Jannik with a **hint** of pride.

"He's got an unfair advantage though, with Jo there to tell him what to do." Nico was right. "Just wait and see how he gets on without him."

It was a glorious day. There was hardly a cloud in the sky; the wind was blowing gently and steadily; and in no time the novices were sailing **jauntily** over the waves.

Isa looked at her watch. "I've got to get back to Florentine," she said. "I'll catch you later, OK?"

She ran along the beach towards the bungalow. There was no one on the patio. Florentine wasn't inside either.

Isa paused. Maybe her aunt had been too hungry to wait? Maybe she'd gone to the clubhouse? Should she go and look for her, or was she worrying unnecessar-

---

to capsize – kentern; to grasp sth – etw. begreifen;
gravity – Schwerkraft; hint – Spur; jauntily – unbeschwert

ily? Oh hell! Isa **felt cross**. Her aunt was always disappearing and she never left a note!

This wasn't the kind of holiday she'd hoped for!

She was still considering what to do, when Florentine hobbled over the patio and into the bungalow. She seemed pleased with herself. "I've got great news!" she shouted.

"Where were you?" said Isa in relief.

Florentine waved a piece of paper at her. "I just went to pick up a fax from reception." She beamed.

"From your ex?"

"No!" Florentine laughed. "From one of my colleagues. We've just won a **contract**. A really big one! I should fly straight back really, but there aren't any seats on these charter flights, damn it!"

"What kind of contract?"

"The Hotel Royal is being renovated, and we've been asked to do the interior design. Imagine that!"

The Hotel Royal was the biggest hotel in town. It was actually a little way out of the centre and was famous for its restaurant as well as for its beautiful **location**, right next to the river.

"Congratulations!" said Isa, giving Florentine a hug.

"And who'll be doing the renovation work?"

Florentine dropped onto the bed. "You've got three guesses!"

"The man with the terrible name," she said immediately. "Bert-Wolfram, the guy you've sent packing. Am I right?"

---

to feel cross – verärgert sein; contract – Auftrag;
location – Lage

Florentine nodded. "It's **ridiculous**," she said, "but what am I supposed to do? I'm not going to back out just because of him. No way."

"Maybe you'll make up again." Isa sat down next to Florentine on the bed.

Florentine closed her eyes and didn't reply.

"Would that be so terrible?"

Florentine hunted for a tissue. "Yes," she said softly, "it certainly would."

"I don't get it," said Isa. "You used to love him. Don't you like him at all any more?"

"I like him a lot," said Florentine slowly. "That's not the problem. It's like this. You know how we were talking about Jannik and Big Macs yesterday?"

Isa nodded.

"Well, Bert-Wolfram had two burgers on the go and was taking the **tastiest** bits out of both. He didn't exactly **shout it from the rooftops**. He just decided for himself and went ahead. And it's the fact that he did it on his own, that's the problem. Like I said, people aren't burgers that you can pick up and consume. When someone notices that they're being treated like a Big Mac, they start protesting and everything comes crashing down. The first person doesn't see what's wrong with their pick 'n' mix tactics, while the other one has to decide whether they like being treated like a burger. If they don't, it's time to say goodbye!"

Isa nodded. "So that's what you did?"

"Well, it took a bit longer than that. At first, I tried

---

ridiculous – lächerlich; tasty – lecker;
to shout sth from the rooftops – etw. an die große Glocke hängen

**reasoning with** him. I told him what the consequences would be."

"And what were they?" asked Isa.

"Listen up! You should write this down too: 'That even the strongest love will die without trust!' But he didn't want to know."

"Why not?"

"No idea. Maybe because he didn't want to miss out on what he calls his 'freedom'. Or maybe he couldn't make up his mind. Then again, perhaps he's happy with loving small bits of people and can't imagine it any other way."

"So what happened next?"

"I told him he had two options: **either** I could accept the existence of the second burger and we could stay together, or I could say goodbye to him ..."

"... and tell him you don't come in pieces; you only come as a whole." Isa finished her sentence for her, thinking of Jannik. "Bingo!"

Florentine laughed. "Exactly! But it took me a while to get to the bingo stage. I'll tell you about that some other time – maybe. Anyway, let's get something to eat. My stomach's rumbling."

---

to reason with sb – vernünftig mit jmd. reden; either – entweder

# The Last-Minute Offer

Later that afternoon Tersia dropped by.

"Your foot's all right now, isn't it, Florentine? That calls for a celebration! You've got to start enjoying life again, and the beach club is the ideal place. The atmosphere is perfect: why not make the most of it?"

Florentine laughed. "So what do you **propose**?"

Tersia dragged her over to the mirror. "Look at yourself! You've got to **smarten yourself up** a bit!"

"**No can do**. I've got absolutely nothing to wear. I came here to have a quiet time, lie in the sun and wait until ... well, until ..."

"What rubbish!" exclaimed Tersia. "You look good when you feel good. And even if you don't feel good, you have to pretend you're the happiest person alive. It's important to make an effort; you've got to dress with **pizazz** and laugh until you drop – and then you'll see what a difference it makes. Laughing is the best medicine for **pent-up** aggression."

"Tersia! How can you be so superficial?"

"I'm not superficial," protested Tersia, "I'm practical. I'm wise to this stuff – I speak from experience."

"I can see that!" Isa taunted her. "Just because

---

to propose – vorschlagen; to smarten oneself up – sich herausputzen; no can do – geht nicht; pizazz – Pep; pent-up – aufgestaut you've got a few **wrinkles,** you think you're the world's leading expert on life and how to lead it."

"What do you know about life, you **spring chicken**, you!" Tersia peered at her reflection in the mirror. "What wrinkles? I don't see any!"

"Try laughing then," Isa challenged her.

"Oh, right!" Tersia shook her golden ringlets. "You nearly got me worried then. Wrinkles! I've **deleted** the word from the dictionary. But seriously, Florentine, you'll come to the clubhouse with me, won't you? I'll lend you something to wear."

"Of course, she will," said Isa. "You can't sneak into bed at nine o'clock again, Florentine. And Tersia will take good care of you, won't you, Tersia?"

"Of course, I will, sweetie. You just go ahead and have a nice evening with your friends. There's no need to worry about anything."

"When you put it like that, I feel worried already," said Isa. "I'll definitely be asking Hugo whether all the boats have been tied up properly ..."

"And whether he's searched the area for sea urchins," added Tersia in peals of laughter.

"Yeah, and he'll need to fence off the Mediterranean in case Florentine falls in!"

"What about the snorkels?" asked Florentine.

"Oh, we almost forgot about them. The snorkels will have to be locked up in an enormous safe, it goes without saying. Now come on, Florentine. Let's see if I've got anything that fits you."

The evening was shaping up nicely for Isa. Tersia was obviously doing her best to help Florentine, but

---

wrinkle – Falte; spring chicken – Küken; to delete – löschen better still, with her aunt now taken care of, Isa was free to write her long-promised letter to Felix. Of course, the letter wouldn't get there until after she was back, but it was the thought that counted.

She started on the opening line and sucked the end of her pen. Should she say "Dear Felix" or just "Hello!"? She decided in favour of a clever combination and wrote: "Hello, dear Felix, shame you're …"

"Are you writing love letters again?"

Isa started. "You never learn, do you? Why can't you knock or let me know that you're coming, like any normal person? I hate the way you ambush me!"

Jannik **hitched up** his baggy trousers with one hand. He was clutching a flower in the other. "It's for you! I wanted to surprise you."

"That doesn't mean you can't knock first. I don't want your **weeds** anyway."

"Now it will shrivel up and die. It's all your fault," said Jannik accusingly.

"What a fuss about nothing …" Isa filled her toothbrush glass with water. "Give it here … Was there anything else you wanted?"

Jannik swallowed. "No. I just wanted to see whether you were ready for dinner, that's all. But if you want to finish your love letter, I can wait."

"How kind of you."

Isa got back to her letter. "… shame you're not here. The weather is amazing and the sea is warm enough …"

"I've been thinking about you," said Jannik.

"You've been doing what?" Isa looked up at him.

---

to hitch up – hochziehen; weed – Unkraut

"Thinking about you."

"And why have you been thinking about me? What makes me so exciting?"

"You really don't care about me, do you?"

She was never going to finish the letter to Felix. Isa put down her notepad and looked at Jannik. "And if I don't, what's the problem? I thought you wanted to be left alone?"

"That's right, but not the way you do it."

Isa threw her pen onto the table and stood up. "Then tell me what it is that you want."

Jannik looked at her unhappily. "If only I knew!"

"Well, I can't help you then. I'm going to the clubhouse. You can come too, if you like."

Isa had no desire to let her last-but-one evening on holiday be ruined by Jannik. They'd only see each other for two more days, and then it would be time to say goodbye and they'd never see each other again. Jannik would have to learn to **deal with** his own problems. Maybe he'd manage it, and maybe not. That was his business ... Isa was already looking forward to going home, to seeing her parents and her little brother and her friends. And she was especially **looking forward** to seeing Astra, 'her' horse, and Felix. She thought again how lucky she was to have such a clear and uncomplicated relationship.

Senta, Amelie and Nico were waiting by the pool.

"Why aren't you in the clubhouse?" asked Isa. "Is nothing happening today?"

---

to deal with – sich mit jmd./etw. befassen;
to look forward – sich auf etw. freuen

"Yeah, there probably is, but look over there ..." Senta pointed to the left. A row of lights were shining down on a **makeshift catwalk**.

Two models in low-cut evening dresses minced forwards. They were wearing wigs – one in bright yellow and the other in orange.

"But that's Hugo and Hans!" Isa burst out laughing as Hugo's fake **bosom** slipped down and poked out beneath the hem of his dress.

"Hans and Hugo as transvestites," said Jannik in a bored voice. He straightened his sunglasses. "How tedious."

"**Spoilsport**," scolded Amelie affectionately. She slipped her arm through his, and pulled him along.

They watched Hugo and Hans until it got dark. Then they wandered around the pool.

"It's a bit early for the disco," said Nico. "Shall we call in at the clubhouse first?"

"What? With the old folks?" asked Amelie. "Whatever turns you on."

"We could just watch for a bit, until things get going in the disco," suggested Nico.

The clubhouse had been decorated to correspond to the Greek islanders' idea of a Hungarian beer-garden. Golden yellow **corn-cobs** dangled from the ceiling together with green vine leaves, black grapes and red Chinese lanterns – all made of the finest plastic. Everyone was on their best behaviour, sitting in tables of four, drinking wine that was so strong it was practically on fire. They raised their green-tinted wine

---

makeshift catwalk – improvisierter Laufsteg; bosom – Busen; spoilsport – Spielverderber; corn-cob – Maiskolben

glasses and listened to the band, which was playing melancholy **tunes**.

"God, it's hilarious," said Nico. He elbowed Jannik: "Look, your dad's sitting over there with Florentine and Tersia."

Florentine was wearing a tiger-print blouse. That's typical Tersia, thought Isa. It doesn't suit Florentine at all.

"They're dying of boredom," said Senta.

"Let's go!" Isa dragged Nico and Amelie towards the door. She'd had enough of her role as aunt-sitter. And the conversations she kept having with Florentine were really **unsettling** ...

"Hang on a minute," said Senta.

A woman was standing next to one of the tables. She took someone's hand, bent over it and looked at it fixedly. She said something to the man, who **shrank back**, pulled his hand away and then offered it to the woman again. She had long black hair and was dressed in a colourful skirt and a white blouse.

"Do you think she's a **gypsy**?" asked Nico. "What's she doing here?"

The woman took the man's hand and gently closed his fingers over his **palm**, as if there was something **valuable** he needed to hold on to. Then she turned around and seemed to be looking for something. Her eyes roved around the room, then she headed for Florentine.

There was a short exchange, and Florentine hesi-

---

tune – Melodie; unsettling – beunruhigend;
to shrink back – zurückweichen; gypsy – Zigeuner;
palm – Handfläche; valuable – wertvoll

tantly held out her right hand. The woman bent over it and traced the lines with her index finger.

Isa and her friends drew closer.

"Things are changing," said the stranger. "At work you are very successful, but in your personal life …"

Florentine snatched back her hand. "I don't want to know," she said fiercely. "I want to decide for myself. It's my decision, and I don't want anything else to affect it."

The stranger nodded in agreement. "You don't need to hear what I was going to tell you. You know already, I can tell." She turned around and walked across the room towards another table.

"What did she want?" asked Isa.

"She's a **fortune-teller**. She reads palms. I didn't call her over," said Florentine. "She was the one who chose me. As if …"

"Why didn't you want to hear any more?" asked Nico **nosily**. "I'd have wanted to. I wouldn't have stopped her. It must be cool to know what's **in store for you**!"

Florentine laughed. "I'd have said that when I was your age too. Why don't you guys take a seat?"

"Thanks, but no thanks!" Isa was bored of the clubhouse already. It was time for some dancing.

In the disco she danced away all the thoughts that were **troubling** her. By the time it got to midnight, her neck was aching and her legs felt as though they didn't belong to her. She was thirsty and she'd sud-

---

fortune-teller – Wahrsagerin; nosily – neugierig;
to be in store for sb – jmd. bevorstehen;
to trouble sb – jmd. beunruhigen

denly had enough of the noise, the cigarette smoke, the heat and the flashing lights.

She waved to Nico, who was standing nearby, and disappeared.

Once she was outside she **took a deep breath** of fresh air. Then she laughed **in spite of** her tiredness. How had Florentine got on? Had Tersia remembered to take good care of her? Was she tucked up in bed asleep? That would be too good to be true – Isa would never **get over** the shock! She quickened her pace.

Red Rose 29, 30, 31. She got to the door, put the key in the lock and pushed.

It was dark inside. She strained her ears. "Florentine?"

She wasn't back yet. Let's just hope, thought Isa, that Tersia's done her job properly and Florentine isn't wandering about in the dark on her own. At least Walter was with them. No, there was no need to worry. Florentine was almost over Bert-Wolfram, and in two days' time – no, tomorrow! – they'd be flying home.

Isa tried not to think about Florentine. She sat out on the patio, thought of Felix and went back inside. She yawned and was about to get undressed when she suddenly felt wide-awake again.

OK, she thought, if I can't get to sleep anyway, I may as well go back to the clubhouse and look for her. If I find her, that's great. If she comes back with me, that's good too. Either way it's better than lying here, waiting for her and imagining what might have happened.

---

to take a deep breath – tief Luft holen;
in spite of – trotz; to get over sth – über etw. hinwegkommen

Isa was surprised at herself. She'd never felt so **responsible** for anyone before. She'd often had to look after her little brother, but that was easy. In fact, that was actually fun.

She was cross with herself for not having called in at the clubhouse in the first place. Now she'd have to go out again, and the path wasn't even lit properly.

A light was shining over an olive tree a little way off. Two people were standing there, giggling.

The man was trying to put his arms around the woman, but she kept **ducking**. Isa couldn't tell whether she was flirting with him or whether she really wasn't interested.

So old and yet so childish, thought Isa. We're much cooler …

She listened. Wasn't that Florentine's voice?

It was Florentine! Isa felt the anger rising up inside her.

If it hadn't been for her **sense of duty**, she'd have been fast asleep in bed by now. Instead, she was out searching for her **accident-prone** aunt, worried that she'd come to some harm. And what had her aunt been doing all this time? Frittering the night away, leant against a gnarled old olive tree, talking to a man.

Isa had had enough of her aunt's mood swings. What was it that she'd said recently? That she was **through with** men? That she didn't want to have anything to do with them again? Obviously, thought

---

responsible – verantwortlich; to duck – sich ducken;
sense of duty – Pflichtbewusstsein; accident-prone – Pechvogel;
to be through with sth – mit etw. fertig sein

Isa, that's how much an adult's word is worth. Thanks a bunch, Florentine.

"Stop!" An arm wound its way around her neck. A hand clamped over her mouth.

She felt herself being pulled backwards, but before she had time to panic, she realized what was happening. There was only one person who would choose such a stupid way of getting her attention ...

"Jannik! What's the matter with you?" she **growled** at him through his fingers.

"Shush! Didn't you see Florentine and my dad over there? Don't **interrupt** them. I had enough trouble trying to get rid of Tersia."

"Why not?" asked Isa in astonishment. "It makes no difference. We're going home tomorrow, and then we'll never see each other again."

"It's not what you think," said Jannik softly, pulling her into the shadow of one of the bungalows. "My dad really likes your aunt. He wants her to relocate and come and work for him."

"I see, so that's what he's after, is it?" Isa said slowly. Oh no, she thought to herself, not another person who thinks he can use his Big-Mac methods to organize his life and loves.

"And so that's what he's busy telling her underneath the olive tree. How romantic! Well, if I know Florentine, she'll never fall for such an idiotic plan."

"What's idiotic about it? She'd stand to gain ..."

Isa pushed Jannik out of the way. "You just don't get it, do you?"

She made a break for the tree, yelling as she ran:

---

to growl – knurren; to interrupt – unterbrechen

"Hi! Florentine! I was worrying about you! I thought you wanted to be back by midnight?"

She drew closer. "Sorry, am I interrupting something?"

"Not at all," said Florentine. "Good night, Walter. I'll see you tomorrow on the beach."

"At ten," Walter reminded her. "Or do you want me to pick you up on the way?"

"No need: my alarm clock's fully functional and so is my watch." Florentine was in **high spirits**. She linked arms with Isa.

"He made you an offer, right?" said Isa once they were **out of earshot**. "You didn't accept, did you?"

Florentine shook her head energetically. "Who do you take me for? It took a lot of hard work to win my **independence**. There's no way I'd give it up now to work for someone else. But how come you know about it anyway?"

"Jannik told me, of course."

Florentine nodded. "Of course."

"And what are you up to tomorrow?"

"Walter wants to show me how brilliantly he can sail a catamaran. Besides, I'm sure he hasn't taken my 'no' very seriously. He probably thinks that if he can get me all alone in a little boat, **surrounded** by water and with no one else around ..."

"... you're bound to accept."

"Exactly."

"But you won't change your mind, will you?" demanded Isa.

---

high spirits – Hochstimmung; out of earshot – außer Hörweite; independence – Unabhängigkeit; surrounded – umgeben

Florentine unlocked the door. “No,” she said firmly. “I’ll tell him we can do things the other way around and he can relocate instead. It’ll be like dripping superglue in his ears. He’ll suddenly become **deaf**, and won’t remember having said anything at all. He’ll deny ever having mentioned the future. Just you wait and see!”

---

deaf – taub

# Room to Manoeuvre

That morning Florentine put on her oldest **swimming costume**. Once upon a time it had been black, but now there was a fine silvery shimmer to it.

"It's like an old person's hair," said Isa. "Don't you think it looks a bit **threadbare**? Why don't you wear your racy new bikini? It would suit you much better."

"I believe in inner beauty," said Florentine, smiling at her reflection in the mirror. "What's a good figure in a sexy bikini really worth? **Zilch**. Anyone can look like one of those pretty girls by the pool so long as they go to the gym and torture themselves from time to time."

"Whereas with inner beauty?"

"Neither money nor **sweat** can guarantee you inner beauty. And you can't get it from a 20 €-session on a sun bed either. You only get inner beauty when **destiny** comes into play."

"Florentine!" exclaimed Isa, aghast. "But everyone has their own destiny."

"Exactly," agreed Florentine unruffled. "But it all depends on what you make of it. Do you know the line from that advert? Some people go through life with a fate-resistant covering: happiness and unhap-

---

swimming costume – Badeanzug; threadbare – abgenutzt; zilch – null; sweat – Schweiß; destiny – Schicksal

piness fall away from them like **droplets** off a Gore-Tex jacket. And do you know why? It's because **fear** makes them cut themselves off from the world."

"I don't get it. Fear of what?"

"Think about it! If you're unhappy, you really hurt."

Isa nodded. "But you don't hurt when you're happy."

"Exactly. But you can always stop being happy, and then it hurts twice as much. That's nobody's idea of fun. Which is why some people retreat into their own private emotional bunker, lock themselves in with their personal pin code and give up on destiny. One path is cowardly; the other one takes courage. But let's not talk about that now. What are you up to today? Do you want to stay here?"

"I'm coming with you," said Isa. "I want to see how Walter deals with the catamaran."

It was much warmer than usual. Jo had already put up a **parasol** and had positioned his little table and chair underneath it. He was giving Walter some final instructions.

"Make sure you don't **collide** with anyone!" said Jo. "Remember that you're on holiday, Walter. There's no need to **compete** or go breaking any records. Take it easy man, OK?"

Walter nodded impatiently and handed Florentine a life jacket. "No problem, Jo. Don't worry – I'm not about to **trash** your boat."

---

droplet – Tröpfchen; fear – Angst; parasol – Sonnenschirm; to collide – zusammenstoßen; to compete – wetteifern; to trash – verwüsten

He pushed the catamaran into the water. "Come on, Florentine, hurry up!" he yelled, and helped her up into the boat.

Florentine turned around towards the shore, gave the victory sign and called out: "Here's to the **coura-geous** women of history, Isa!"

The wind filled the catamaran's sails and it sped away.

Isa fetched a deckchair and sat next to Jo under the parasol. She was cross with herself for not bringing her notepad: it was the perfect place to sit and de-scribe the bay. The catamarans were stirring up the silvery blue water as they **whizzed past** with their colourful sails. Some of the surfers stood confidently on their boards while others wobbled **precariously**. A water-skier blazed a trail through the waves and lit-tle kids were talking excitedly about the next **crucial** stages in their sand-building plans ...

"There you are! I've been looking for you every-where," said Jannik, plumping himself down next to Isa. "You're impossible! Why did you and Florentine run off like that last night? I don't get it. I thought we said we'd try to pair them up." He pushed his sun-glasses into his carroty-orange hair.

"Don't look at me so **accusingly**," complained Isa. "I'm not your pet robot; I'm human, OK?"

"I know, but I still don't understand why you ran off like that."

What was the point of trying to explain that kind of thing to Jannik? It would be as new to him as sun-

---

courageous – tapfer; to whiz past – vorbeijagen; precariously – unsicher; crucial – entscheidend; accusingly – anklagend stroke to an Inuit. But that wasn't the only problem: even if she managed to explain it, he'd never understand. Isa fell silent.

"Why are you so quiet?"

She stretched out her legs, leant back and looked at him.

Jannik went red.

"Tomorrow," said Isa, "we'll be flying home."

"That's exactly it," said Jannik. "Tomorrow it will all be over."

"I should have thought you'd be pleased," teased Isa. "Tomorrow evening you'll have your peace and quiet again. There'll be no one there to make your life **awkward**. You won't have to put up with anyone doing the wrong thing or asking you questions like, 'How's it going? What have you been up to? What did you think of the island?'. No one will expect you to give any answers. Wow, the good, old days of utter detachment will be back. You must be really looking forward to it."

"That's what you think!" Jannik looked out over the water. "And what will you be doing tomorrow evening?"

"My parents will be there to meet us at the airport. We'll have dinner together and talk and talk and talk. My parents have been away in Tuscany and my little brother Paul has been on a camping holiday – sleeping in a tent, eating worms and **beetles**, not having washed for a week. And if I start describing Florentine's long list of accidents, we're sure to be up all night!"

---

awkward – schwierig; beetle – Käfer

"Lucky you," said Jannik.

"It's easy to say that!" Isa flashed him a look. "You wouldn't **survive** in my family. We've got rules, see, and we stick to them."

Jannik looked at her **enquiringly**.

"Well, the first rule is: don't keep secrets!"

"Having to tell everyone all about yourself – how awful!"

"I told you it wouldn't be your thing," said Isa. "My family isn't as **laid-back** as yours. Even so, we don't wind each other up by continually asking what the others are thinking, feeling or planning. In fact, exactly the opposite."

"I don't get it."

"Not keeping secrets, in our family that means –" Isa thought for a moment. "It means we can trust each another because we never do anything that would **offend** or hurt the others, not even behind their back. That's much better than just being helped out in emergencies or when you're in trouble with a teacher and you suddenly need your parents for support. I've got a lot more freedom than my friends. But when my parents think something is bad for me, they **intervene** – big time!" Isa laughed and explained about her tutor. "So you see," she added, "if my parents hadn't known about my bad marks, they wouldn't have been able to help in time, and I would have had to repeat the year – and that wouldn't have been good for anyone, would it?"

---

to survive – überleben; enquiringly – fragend;
laid-back – locker; to offend – beleidigen;
to intervene – einmischen

"You said that you're allowed to do much more than your friends. I bet that's not true."

"I didn't say I was allowed to do more. I said I had more 'freedom'. My parents trust me because they know I won't use my freedom to do things they wouldn't **approve of.**"

"Hang on a minute. What do you mean?"

"Why do you want to know?" **teased** Isa. "Why are you so interested all of a sudden? You're usually happy **to settle for** half of anything. Now it's your turn to explain!"

"I don't think so."

"Fair enough."

Someone tripped over Isa's outstretched legs.

"Sorry," said Tersia. "I didn't mean to interrupt. It sounds as if you're in the middle of an important debate."

"Too right," said Jannik quickly. "Isa was telling me about her family and how they don't keep secrets."

"My God!" exclaimed Tersia. "Are you all **saints** or something? Life without secrets is like soup without salt: **nutritious**, but incredibly boring!"

"That's what I was saying," Jannik agreed.

Isa shrugged. "You don't know what you're talking about, but you're happy to **judge** as if you had all the details."

"Do we need any details?" demanded Tersia. "The fact that you don't keep secrets is enough for me! I've

---

to approve of sth – etw. gutheißen; to tease – necken;
to settle for sth – mit etw. zufrieden sein; saint – Heilige(r);
nutritious – nahrhaft; to judge – urteilen

got countless secrets. Secrets are really important to me: they give me **room to manoeuvre**. I need them to stop people from grabbing hold of me, pinning me up on the wall and hanging a sign over my head: 'Tersia – small, light-weight model, high-quality goods with a glossy finish.' I want to enjoy life. And the only way I can do that is by keeping secrets." Tersia laughed. "I like life to be exciting and full of surprises."

"And what happens when you find someone to **share** it with?" asked Isa, thinking of Florentine and her ex-boyfriend, the schmuck who had caused her such trouble.

"Someone? I hope I never have to settle for one!"

Jo came back and glanced at his watch. "They've been out for a long time," he said disapprovingly. He reached for his **binoculars**.

He scanned the water. "They're a long way out. It's about time they turned around and came back in again ... It looks as though Walter is having trouble turning. There, he's trying to turn now ... he's still trying ... still trying ... What's he playing at? He doesn't seem to be able to do it. Come on, man, try turning the other way! ... That's right, that's the way to do it."

Jo lowered his binoculars. "The wind is much stronger out there," he explained. "Walter hasn't got any feel for the boat yet, he's got to ..."

He looked through the binoculars again. "Oh no!

---

room to manoeuvre – Freiraum;
to share – teilen;
binoculars – Fernglas

What's he doing now? I can't believe it! The boat's leaning over to one side. If he's not careful, he'll catch a **gust** and it'll all be over. Hopefully, he's clever enough to ... No! Sh... Damn!"

Isa leapt to her feet. "What's up? What's going on?"

"Take a look for yourself!" Jo tossed her the binoculars.

"I can't see anything!" Isa fumbled with the settings. "Oh God, they've capsized! You've got to save them, Jo!"

"Let's wait and see whether they manage it on their own." He took the binoculars out of her hand. "Walter knows what to do in order to get the boat back up again. The big question is: will he manage it? Florentine won't be much help."

"Great. I wish Walter had capsized with me onboard," exclaimed Tersia. "Then I'd have something to tell my friends back home."

Jo growled under his breath. He stared through the binoculars.

"That's right," he said with satisfaction. "They've swum around to the right side ... But what's Florentine up to? She's carried on swimming! I think she's heading for shore. That's crazy – she'll never make it! That's the first and most important rule of sailing: never move away from the boat!"

"How's Florentine supposed to know?" Isa defended her aunt. "Besides, she's a really strong swimmer."

"It's easy to **underestimate** the distance," replied

---

gust [of wind] – Böe;
to underestimate – unterschätzen

Jo. "Do you know how difficult it is to spot someone's head in the water? ... Phew, she's swimming back towards Walter."

"And my dad?" asked Jannik. "What's my dad doing?"

"He's ... he's doing it right! He's doing exactly the right thing!" shouted Jo enthusiastically. "He's holding on to the side, he's pulling ... Pull harder!" he yelled, as if Walter could hear him. "Go on, pull, pull, yes! That's right! Just a little bit more, a little bit more and pull! ... Give it some welly! Don't stop now. Give it all you've got! Yesss! ... No! Nooooo!"

Jo chucked the binoculars onto the table. "He's not going to do it on his own. I'm going to have to go out and help them. I'll need another man to come along and **lend a hand**."

"A man? Why not a woman? Take me!" offered Tersia.

Jo made a **telling** gesture with his hands. "Are you coming?" he said to Jannik, and ran off towards his motorboat without waiting for an answer. He jumped in and started the motor.

Jannik had no choice but to follow.

"My God, this is exciting!" said Tersia with delight. "If it weren't for Florentine, things would be really dull around here. But she's a real **gift**. There's always something going on when she's around!"

"Who's a gift?" Hugo suddenly appeared alongside them.

Tersia giggled. "You, of course. I've been missing you terribly."

---

to lend a hand – helfen; telling – viel sagend; gift – Geschenk

"Rubbish," said Hugo. "What's going on here? I was over at the jetty when someone ran up to tell me that Jo needs my help. Where he's got to?"

Isa pointed out to sea.

"Where?"

Tersia linked arms with Hugo and rested her head on his shoulders. "It's a matter of life and death," she said, rolling her eyes. "Walter and Florentine have sailed out to sea."

Hugo **disentangled himself** and reached for the binoculars. "Have they capsized? Is that them over there?"

"Calm down," said Tersia. "They're about to be rescued by Jo and Jannik."

"Besides, Florentine's a really good swimmer," said Isa stubbornly.

In her view, everyone was making a fuss about nothing. No doubt, Jo just wanted to throw his weight around and show everyone how proficient he was.

Hugo looked at her despairingly. "What did I tell you? Didn't I say that Florentine should be locked in a tower until it's time for her to leave? It's for her own **benefit** and for the benefit of everyone else in the club! But no one listens to me!"

"Florentine isn't Rapunzel!" shrieked Isa. "We don't live in fairyland, you know! And in any case, you'll be pleased to hear that we're flying home tomorrow. Tomorrow's our last day."

Hugo looked at her in surprise. "Well, that's a **relief**," he said gloomily.

---

to disentangle oneself from sth – sich von etw. befreien; for the benefit of sb – zu jmds. Nutzen; relief – Erleichterung

Isa couldn't help laughing. "You can start counting the hours till we go: you've only got the rest of this morning, this afternoon, this evening and tomorrow morning. Surely nothing else can happen now."

"With Florentine anything's possible, don't you think, Hugo?" Tersia winked at him.

Hugo didn't notice because he was still staring through the binoculars.

Isa started to get worried. "Is something wrong?"

"Jo's there now. He's showing them what to do ... Walter is **clinging** onto the boat and Florentine's clinging onto him ... The sail's lifting out of the water! Perfect! ... No! Nooooo! Oh God!"

"What is it?"

"They managed to **right** the boat, but then it toppled over and fell down on top of them. I hope they haven't hurt themselves ... No, there they are. They've swum underneath it and come up the other side."

"And now what?"

"Jo's jumped into the water. He's helping Walter. They've done it! Yep, they've righted the boat again! Walter is climbing in while Jo holds onto the side ... Good!"

"What's Florentine doing?"

"Walter's helping her up ... Why doesn't she come back in the motorboat?"

"Because she's brave," said Isa in satisfaction. "Pass me the binoculars."

She adjusted them, and then watched Jo climbing back into the motorboat. He waited until Walter and

---

to cling – klammern; to right sth – etw. aufrichten

Florentine had sorted out the sails and the ropes. The sails filled with wind.

Jo and Jannik drove alongside the catamaran until it reached the shore. The sand crunched under the **keel**. They sprang into the shallow water. They'd made it.

"Florentine!" yelled Isa. "I'm not going to let you out of my sight! Are you OK?"

Florentine laughed. "I'm fine! Now I know why you need a life jacket!"

"Why did you capsize? Was the wind too strong?"

"Well, it *was* quite **breezy** out there, but the wind wouldn't have been enough to blow us over. It was only when Walter's mobile went off and he went to answer it ..."

"He had his mobile with him?" asked Hugo incredulously.

"Well, of course! He'd put it in a plastic bag to keep it safe! Anyway, someone was calling Walter, he tried to answer, he dropped the rudder and a gust of wind came and blew us over. And that was that. Thanks for rescuing us."

"It'll cost you a bottle of champagne," said Jo. "Jannik, why don't you run and get one. We'll wait here and sort out some glasses."

"Is that really what happened?" probed Hugo. "I can't believe it. Oh well, at least you're back safely."

Tersia draped her towel around Walter's shoulders. "You poor thing, you're freezing." She rubbed the water off his back and winked at the others. "What are you going to do without your mobile?"

---

keel – Kiel; breezy – windig

Walter had the situation under control. "Without it? Don't worry – I've got a **spare**."

"That's right, Walter, don't worry about **endangering** yourself or Florentine – protecting your electronic **umbilical cord** is much more important!" said Hugo sarcastically. "Florentine, you should stick with me for the rest of today. I'd been planning to ask you whether you fancied going on a trip this afternoon anyway. Isa, do you want to come too?"

Isa played with the ring in her belly button. "Where are you going?"

"I'd like to show you the old town and the bazaar."

"Old town? Bazaar? But we're on a **tiny** island." Isa looked sceptical.

"It's not that tiny. The town is actually quite big, and the old part of it is really pretty and full of winding streets. You'll like it there. But please, Florentine, make sure you stay with me. If you get lost, you'll have trouble finding your way through all the little **alleyways.**"

"Don't worry: I think I've had enough excitement for one day."

"I haven't." Tersia played with her hair. "A thrilling new adventure is exactly what I need on my very last day. Can I come too?"

Walter cleared his throat. "I'll join you."

Jo laughed. "I'm not sure that's what you **had in mind**, was it, Hugo? Maybe you should go ahead and invite the whole beach club!"

---

spare – Reserve; to endanger – gefährden;
umbilical cord – Nabelschnur; tiny – winzig;
alleyway – Gasse; to have in mind – an etw. denken

Hugo shook his head. Then he put his arm around Florentine and said: "You can all come. We'll leave the minibus at the car park and go our own separate ways from there. We can meet again later."

"Good, we're happy with that, aren't we, Florentine?" said Walter.

"Hang on a minute. I never said I wanted to go with you." Florentine glared at Walter angrily.

"Come on, people, don't get upset. You're supposed to be on holiday," said Jo. He took the bottle out of Jannik's hand. "Let's **bury our differences** and have a drink. **Cheers**!"

"So when are we setting off?" Tersia asked Hugo. "It will take me a while to get ready."

"Five o'clock at reception."

"Bye then! See you later!"

---

to bury differences – Meinungsverschiedenheiten beiseite lassen; Cheers! – Prost!

# Emotions

Florentine **peeled off** her wet swimming costume and took a warm shower.

"Did you see that?" she shouted from the bathroom. "We were pushing and pulling out there, not knowing whether we'd be able to get the boat up, but no one came to help us. They must have seen our sail in the water for miles off. It's bright enough! But the other catamarans took one look and sailed off."

"Were you scared?"

"Not especially. I couldn't help wondering how long it would take before anyone noticed we were gone. The water was really **chilly** ... But Walter was so worked up! All he could think about was his wretched mobile. I told him he should look for it on the bottom. A little deep-sea diving never hurt anyone!" Florentine laughed.

There was a knock at the door.

"Hang on a minute!" yelled Isa, hastily pulling on a long skirt and her T-shirt with the swirls.

"A fax for Florentine!" It was Karen from reception. "I can't wait to meet her – the whole club's been talking about your aunt and her **antics**! They're looking forward to the next **instalment**!"

---

to peel off – abstreifen; chilly – kalt; antics – Eskapaden; instalment – Folge/Fortsetzng

"What next instalment?" Florentine emerged from the bathroom, wrapped in a towel.

"Hi there! You look thoroughly drowned. Oh well, I guess all the excitement is good for the club. A fax has just arrived for you. See you around ..."

Florentine skimmed the fax and handed it to Isa. "Looking forward to working with you. Love, Bert-Wolfram."

"What more could you ask for?" asked Isa, putting the fax on the coffee-table. "I guess that's all sorted then."

"God, how I hate that man!" said Florentine softly. "He's so unbelievably **thick-skinned**. Why can't he just leave me alone? And I was almost starting to feel all right again."

"I don't see what the problem is," said Isa. "He's only talking about working together, right? What's wrong with that?"

"Am I interrupting something?" Tersia walked in through the open patio door. She stared at the fax. She looked like a stray cat that had just spotted a pot of fresh cream. "Oh! You know Bert-Wolfram, do you?"

Florentine whipped away the sheet of paper. She couldn't hide her surprise. "What? Do you know him too? How come?"

"Is he your neighbour? An **acquaintance**? Or maybe a special friend?" probed Tersia, avoiding the question.

"What's that got to do with you?" asked Isa in surprise.

---

thick-skinned – dickhäutig;
acquaintance – Bekannte(r)

"Oh," said Tersia. "It's just I know him quite well. So what do you think of him, Florentine?"

"He used to be a friend of mine." Florentine was combing her wet hair. Suddenly she stopped. She put the comb down carefully as if it were incredibly **fragile**. "Yes, that's what he was, a friend," she said.

"You sound really angry with him," said Tersia, astonished. "What don't you like about him? I think he's really sweet."

Isa's ears pricked up. "Watch out, Florentine!" she said. "You shouldn't tell her anything." Isa remembered what Tersia had said on the beach. "Tersia likes secrets. She thinks life without them is dreary and boring. Let her find out for herself."

Florentine gave Tersia a searching look. Then she laughed and asked: "Is that true? So you like secrets, do you, Tersia? Then Bert-Wolfram is the man for you."

"Why?"

"Do you really want to know? Is it important to you?"

"You bet!"

"OK, well, I'll tell you. But before that you have to explain where and when you met Bert-Wolfram and what you want from him. That's only fair, don't you think?"

Tersia hesitated.

Suddenly Isa realized why Florentine was offering a deal. Tersia was new in town, she knew Bert-Wolfram and she wanted to find out more about him. If Tersia was going to settle for one man, maybe she could be Bert-Wolfram's blonde!

---

fragile – zerbrechlich

"My God, Tersia," said Florentine impatiently. "It was you who wanted to hear about him. He's got nothing to do with me any more."

"Right, I'll tell you …" Tersia wrapped one of her long blonde ringlets around her finger. "Well, it was …" She **frowned**, as if she was trying to think.

"You look as though you're trying to **concoct** the most enormous lie," said Isa. "Why would you want to do that? Is it your idea of fun, or are you trying to trick Florentine? I have to look after my aunt, you know."

Tersia gave an embarrassed laugh. "I'm not trying to hurt her."

"That's what you say, but what makes you think we'll agree with you? You've got no right to decide what may or may not hurt Florentine. You're only thinking of yourself."

"OK, OK, Isa, calm down. I can fight my own battles," said Florentine.

"But that's just it: you can't! You don't know what she's like! She's only interested in enjoying her life and she doesn't care about yours. Be careful what you say!"

"What's got into you, Isa? It's not like you to be so **rude**."

"I'm not being rude," protested Isa. "It's just I've learnt to be **wary**, and I wanted to warn you."

"Right, well, you've warned me. But it really wasn't necessary because Bert-Wolfram …"

---

to frown – die Stirn runzeln;
to concoct sth – sich etw. ausdenken; rude – unhöflich;
wary – vorsichtig

"Don't say it!" yelled Isa. "How do you know she won't **twist your words**?"

"Right, that's enough, Isa!" said Florentine vigorously. "I get the feeling that something happened between the two of you while I was being rescued. What's this all about?"

Isa looked at Tersia. "Go on, you tell her."

"Tell her what? But nothing happened. We had a little **chat**, that's all. You know how it is, Florentine. At Isa's age, girls are just one big bundle of emotions. When I think back to when I was fifteen or sixteen … I always saw everything in the blackest of black or the whitest of white. You must have **got the wrong end of the stick**, Isa."

Isa leapt to her feet. "Great. So now I've got the wrong end of the stick, I see everything in black and white and I'm a bundle of emotions – that's just perfect!"

"Isa! What's wrong with you?"

"Maybe we should talk about it another time," said Tersia. "I'll see you at lunch, OK?"

Isa and Florentine watched her go. "So what's wrong, Isa?" said Florentine, hoping for an answer.

Isa struggled to put her **indignation** into words. "Well," she said hesitantly, "it was like this. I was stupid enough to tell Jannik that we have rules in our family, like, for example, not keeping secrets."

Florentine nodded. "That's how your mother and I were brought up too."

---

to twist your words – dir die Worte im Mund herumdrehen; chat – Gespräch; to get the wrong end of the stick – etw. missverstehen; indignation – Empörung

"Well, Jannik started **poking fun at** me because of it, and then Tersia came up and started poking fun at me too. The worst thing was that I never got around to explaining it properly. They didn't give me a chance. They just weren't interested. Now I can't be bothered any more. Everyone's different, I know."

Florentine thought for a moment. Then she took a deep breath and said: "I expect Tersia was brought up to think that she could get away with stuff if she **kept her cards to her chest**. Secrets are nothing out of the ordinary for her. She doesn't think there's anything wrong with ..."

"That's not true!" exclaimed Isa. "She knows it's wrong, otherwise she wouldn't have been so embarrassed. She wouldn't have disappeared like that either. And she wouldn't have tried to make me look **unreliable**," said Isa indignantly. "You only do that kind of thing when you think you're **being cornered**."

"Well, I suppose you might be right," admitted Florentine.

She fell silent while she thought things over. Suddenly her stomach gave such a loud rumble that it made them both jump. They burst out laughing.

Florentine got up. "Come on, let's get some food. But before we go, I've got another piece of advice for you to write down."

"I can hardly wait!"

"Now you're being cheeky again!" said Florentine.

---

to poke fun at sb – sich über jmd. lustig machen;
to keep one's cards to one's chest – sich nicht in die Karten schauen lassen; unreliable – unzuverlässig;
to be cornered – in die Enge getrieben werden

"Well, here it goes: 'Don't go advertising your **treasured** family traditions on the beach'."

Isa nodded. "I've learnt my lesson. But what do you think about secrets?"

Florentine gave Isa a serious look. "It all depends on how close you are to the other person and what that person means to you. At work you have to get used to the fact that everyone has their own agenda. It's just the way it is. But living with someone who's **selfish** enough to keep secrets is an absolute nightmare. It's dreadful to be stuck with someone who lives their life at your expense – unless, of course, you're equally selfish in return." She grinned. "From that point of view Tersia and Bert-Wolfram were made for each other!"

There was another knock at the door.

"That must be Jannik. It's a miracle he hasn't shown up before," said Isa. She opened up.

"One flower for Florentine and one flower for Isa!" Tersia beamed and held out two yellow-coloured blossoms. "Are you still mad at me?"

"You bet," said Isa.

"Oh Tersia, you're impossible," said Florentine. "But you know that already."

Tersia rocked backwards and forwards. "I'm not half as bad as you think. I'm actually just a nice, **straight-forward** girl who ..."

Florentine cut her short: "That might work on the men, but we women know better."

"Oh, of course," said Tersia, as if the thought had

---

treasured – hoch geschätzt; selfish – selbstsüchtig; straight-forward – unkompliziert

never occurred to her. "Can I ask you something about Bert-Wolfram?"

Florentine nodded.

"Have you known each other for long? How well do you know him?"

"Hang on a minute," said Florentine. "How long have *you* known him?"

"Let me see … It must be a couple of months now, or maybe a little longer …" said Tersia vaguely.

"Or maybe even longer than that. How about since last autumn?"

"How do you know?" Tersia bent down to **tighten** her sandals.

"None of your business. I know what I know," said Florentine brutally. "Let's leave it there, shall we? In any case, I'm hungry. How about we go to lunch?"

Isa walked on ahead. I've never met anyone quite like Tersia, she thought. She's completely **unpredictable**. I never know what she'll say next. She really **stirs** things **up** … I've met some really interesting people while I've been here. In fact, it's exactly the way Florentine promised it would be. I could spend all day doing sport, if I wanted to. I've had lots of new experiences and I'm seeing things from a totally different **angle**. The problem is, it's really unsettling. I never knew adults had problems they couldn't deal with. Do my parents have problems too? I used to think they had everything sorted on the emotional front. How awful if I were to get home and everything had changed …

---

to tighten – enger schnallen; unpredictable – unberechenbar; to stir up – aufmischen; angle – Winkel

## New Experiences

After lunch Isa went water-skiing with her friends for the very last time. The wind was stronger than usual and a fine layer of white cloud **veiled** the sky. The sun was hidden behind the haze.

"Look how big the waves are," said Jannik to Isa.

Hugo turned around to look at them. "If they get any bigger, you won't be able to go out. Only experienced skiers can handle conditions like these."

"You mean experienced skiers like you," said Amelie. "I wish I could ski as well as you can."

"Now don't go getting **envious**. Hugo's a natural. And quite apart from that, he spends the entire summer doing nothing but water-skiing," said Nico.

Hugo laughed. "Come on, Nico, you go first! Don't be a coward."

"Hey! I don't need this stress!" Nico hitched up his board shorts and got ready to go. He started perfectly and then **swung** from side to side, cutting elegant curves through the water.

"He's really good," said Isa. She lay down on the jetty, put her hands under her head and closed her eyes. Someone bent over her and tweaked her belly-button ring. "Get out of my sun," she said sleepily.

---

to veil – verschleiern; envious – neidisch;
to swing – schwingen

"Isa," whispered Jannik.

"Hmm?"

"Will you write to me?"

"I don't know. Will you write to me?"

"Yes, all the time. Every single day," he replied.

"Don't bother."

"Why?"

"Because I can't read that much."

"Then I'll call you," he suggested.

"Don't be silly. I'm hardly ever at home. And my parents aren't too keen on long phone calls."

Jannik fell silent.

"You don't like me," he said after a while.

Oh God, thought Isa, what do I say now? She couldn't very well say, "I like you a bit". It would be more honest to tell him that his Big-Mac approach to life reminded her exactly of Bert-Wolfram, but Jannik wouldn't know what she was talking about. **Instead** she said: "I've got a boyfriend, remember?"

"So what? It's not like you'd have to tell him."

That's exactly it, thought Isa. He's exactly like Bert-Wolfram. "Now you're getting on my nerves," she said. "**Give me a break**."

"Do you need some time to think?"

"Nope."

"Too bad."

Isa rolled over onto her tummy and propped herself up on her elbows. "Why don't you find someone else? Someone who actually lives near you. It's much more practical that way. You'll save yourself the tele-

---

instead – stattdessen;
Give me a break! – Lass mich in Ruhe!

phone bills and the **stamps**, and all kinds of other stuff."

"I don't need your advice."

"Good. So you won't keep pestering me then."

"You're heartless. Cold and heartless." Jannik got up.

Hugo was towing Nico towards the jetty. "Well done," he praised him. "Who wants to go next?"

"Me," said Jannik with a steely expression. He took off his sunglasses and got himself ready.

"Watch out, the water feels different today," Nico warned him. "If you're not careful, the waves will knock you over."

"Well, let them ..."

"Are you ready?" shouted Hugo. "Let's get going, OK?"

Jannik got off to a perfect start.

"What's got into him?" demanded Nico. "Has he been having trouble with his dad again?"

No one answered. Nico sat down next to Isa. "Will I see you later?" he asked softly.

"No go. I won't be around."

"But it's your last night!" protested Nico. "You can't just go off somewhere else."

"I'm not just going off somewhere else. I'm going to the bazaar."

"I've been there already. It's good – lots of little shops and **nooks and crannies** and stuff. Do you want to buy some souvenirs? I'll come too, if you like. How are you getting there?"

---

stamp – Briefmarke;
nooks and crannies – Ecken und Winkel

"Hugo's driving us."

"Us? Who's us?"

"Florentine, Walter, Jannik, Tersia and me."

"That's practically a party! If Hugo's got room in the car, I'm coming too."

"Cool," said Isa. "Now where's my towel got to? I'm getting cold."

The sky was completely covered over, and the wind was stronger and colder than ever. Fine droplets of water rose up over the jetty like spray from an **aerosol**.

"There'll be no more water-skiing for you, Isa," said Nico sorrowfully. "It's too bad the weather had to change on your very last day. If I'd known it was going to do that, I'd have let you go first."

"How very noble of you," Isa teased him.

"Well, what do you expect from a **well-brought-up** guy like me?" joked Nico.

Isa laughed. "At least I know where I am with you. You're a breath of fresh air."

"What?" Nico touched her belly-button ring.

"You know, **compared with** Jannik."

Nico let go of the ring. "Things are really hard for him," he said seriously. "He's really bothered by his dad, and it's just the two of them at home together. Jannik shops, cooks and does all the washing. They've got a cleaner, but that doesn't exactly make up for it. He's forgotten how to laugh. He has enough trouble just getting by."

"How do you know?" asked Isa.

---

aerosol – Spraydose; well-brought-up – gut erzogen; compared with – im Vergleich zu

"I called around one night, but his dad was so depressed that he didn't want to leave him on his own. I called in again on my way back from the disco and brought him some juice and something to eat. That's when he told me." Nico looked embarrassed.

"And I've been so mean to him," said Isa guiltily. "The thing is, he can ... well, he ... He never listens to me."

"He can be a pain, I know." Nico helped Isa to her feet. "There they are already. Jannik, what are you doing in the boat?" he shouted.

"He's totally crazy." Hugo was seriously cross. "You can't ski slalom on waves like that. You don't have to be a genius to figure that out. So what does Jannik do? He tries to ski slalom. And then he's surprised when he hits the water. Count yourself lucky!" he barked at Jannik. "It could have been a lot worse. Lie down with some **cold compresses**, OK?"

Jannik hauled himself out of the boat and climbed **unsteadily** up the little ladder to the jetty.

Hugo flung the skis after him. He was furious. "That's it for today, folks. Look at the **windsock**. See the red flag on the beach over there by the catamarans? That means NO MORE watersports."

"OK!" yelled Nico. "I'll see you later!"

"Really? Who said you could come along?"

Nico gave himself a tap on the shoulder. "Sometimes you have to take your fate into your own hands," he said cheekily. "Happiness is like a galloping horse. There's no time for **hesitation**: you have to

---

cold compress – kalter Umschlag; unsteadily – unsicher; windsock – Windsack; hesitation – Unentschlossenheit

grab the reins and fling yourself onto its back. That's what my grandma says."

"She must be a very clever lady," said Hugo, "even if she doesn't have a clue about sport."

"Hey, you're right," said Nico in surprise. "How did you know that?"

"Well, it's no good flinging yourself **willy-nilly** onto the back of a galloping horse. If you're not careful, you'll fall straight off the other side. It takes a lot of practice. You should tell her that."

"I will!"

They all laughed.

Hugo waved goodbye and steered the boat towards the shore.

Jannik hugged his belly.

"What happened?" asked Isa. "Why's your stomach so red?"

Nico put his arm around his shoulders. "Did you hit the water? Does it hurt? Can you walk back all right?"

"I'm fine."

"We'll come with you," said Isa. "OK?"

No one said anything as they walked with Jannik back to his room. Once Jannik had disappeared inside, Isa said: "You know, the thing about your grandma's horse? I mean, what your grandma said about the horse? I liked that. Florentine's always giving me **sayings** to write down and ..."

Nico looked at her in disbelief. "You don't keep a book full of sayings, do you? My little sister's got a

---

willy-nilly – aufs Geratewohl;
sayings – Sprüche

notebook where she writes down sayings. She never lets it out of her sight."

"Oh, I've got a notebook for sayings too, but I never use it. Sometimes I write Florentine's sayings in my diary, sometimes I write them in one of my school books. Sometimes I just forget them. They're not really sayings – they're just things that she thinks are important and that might be useful to me."

"My grandma says you always have to learn for yourself, but that doesn't mean you need to drown yourself in every puddle. Sometimes you need someone to point you in the right direction."

They stood on the beach and looked out over the water. The sky was still clouded over and the waves were crowned with crests of spray. The wind was coming in from the sea. It swept the hair out of their faces.

The catamarans were tied up on the beach. Jo was out in his motorboat, **herding** the last remaining surfers towards the shore. Hugo put a sign up, telling everyone that swimming was forbidden.

Isa said goodbye to Nico, and stepped over the patio wall. She picked up Florentine's costume, her bikini and some towels that they'd left out to dry. She carried them inside.

Florentine was sleeping. Isa tried not to make any noise as she hunted for her notepad and pen. She sat down outside. The air smelt of water, salt and **seaweed**. Isa looked out towards the sea. She was enjoying being on her own, listening to the sound of the waves and the wind. In one hour they were supposed

---

to herd – treiben; seaweed – Seegras

to meet Hugo. Would the weather get any better by then?

She read through her last entry: “Snorkelling.” Only a few days had passed since then, but she’d had so many new experiences! “When you’re underwater you have to use sign-language. It’s not the place to talk or listen.” She smiled to herself. She thought about all the trouble she’d had trying to explain about secrets. There’d been plenty of talking and listening, but Jannik and Tersia still hadn’t understood. And it wouldn’t have been any better even if she’d used sign-language. They’d never understand.

Maybe getting on well with your family could be dangerous too. You feel protected and understood, and then you think everyone else is just as nice and would never mean you any **harm**. Maybe coming from a **stable** home meant you weren’t very well equipped for life. Isa bit her lip. It probably depended on how **sheltered** you were and whether you got to know about other people’s problems. At home she hadn’t taken Florentine’s break-up very seriously. It was only after they’d gone away together that she realized how hard Florentine was fighting to keep it all together.

She still needed to find out what it was that Florentine had found so hurtful. Hopefully, she’d have the chance to ask her – maybe that evening, when they were back from the bazaar.

She definitely wouldn’t have time beforehand. In half an hour they had to be ready … Isa noticed that a thick layer of black cloud had been blown in by the

---

harm – Schaden; stable – stabil; sheltered – geschützt

wind. The clouds were speeding across the sky, **piling up** one after the other, then breaking apart, before racing off again. But there wasn't any rain in sight. And in any case, neither of them had brought an umbrella.

---

to pile up – sich anhäufen

# Hidden Treasures

At five o'clock they were standing at the main entrance to the club: Hugo, Walter, Florentine, Isa, Jannik and Nico.

"We're still waiting for Tersia," said Florentine.

"There she is," exclaimed Nico. "She's all dressed up for the **occasion**."

She was wearing her leather trousers with the lurid green braces. Her golden ringlets gleamed over her tight black top. She'd made liberal use of her perfume.

"Hurry up and get on the bus," Hugo **chivvied** them **along**. "Who knows when the storm will break?"

"Maybe we should stay here," said Florentine. "There's no point in walking around in the rain."

"It won't be that bad," said Hugo. "Are you all **strapped in**? Then let's get going!"

He drove at high speed, so it only took thirty minutes to get into town.

"Let's all walk together to the old town where the bazaar is," suggested Hugo. He led the way and stopped outside a café. "Shall we meet back here in two hours' time? Is that OK with everyone?"

If Hugo had been hoping to spend a couple of

---

occasion – Anlass; to chivvy sb along – jmd. antreiben; strapped in – angeschnallt hours on his own with Florentine, he was soon to be disappointed. No one made the slightest attempt to explore the bazaar on their own. The whole group remained hot on his heels. They slipped in among the mass of people and walked down the **narrow** streets.

They saw **tailors** sitting at their sewing machines in tiny little rooms, then arches filled with bags, cases and holdalls in all shapes and sizes.

Tersia started to rummage through them. The others carried on without her, and she followed them, protesting loudly.

They stopped at a **stall** selling sweets, and bought sugared almonds, candied fruits and cubes of an unidentifiable kind of jelly, coated in icing sugar. Alongside it was a table covered in herbs and **spices**, as well as a special kind of paste labelled "Sultan's Delight" that claimed to be a sure way of making you more **virile**.

"Wait for me," giggled Tersia, her eyes lighting up. She bought several tubes at once, stuffing them into her bag.

The next alley was full of stalls selling **jewellery**. They stood and stared; then they tried on ring after ring, slipped **bangles** over their wrists, stroked the smooth surface of big chunks of amber, admired the shiny coral **pendants**, experimented with different necklaces, and dangled beautifully engraved earrings from their ears.

"I could spend all day here," sighed Isa. She count-

---

narrow – schmal; tailor – Schneider; stall – Verkaufsstand; spice – Gewürz; virile – potent; jewellery – Schmuck; bangle – Armreif; pendant – Anhänger

ed her money, then bought a pair of silver earrings with tiny turquoise droplets. “Do you like them?” she asked Jannik, who was standing right beside her.

He lifted up his sunglasses. “They really suit you,” he said. “Look! There’s even a **matching** ring.”

“I’ve run out of money,” said Isa regretfully. She rummaged through a box of red disks inscribed with **mysterious** signs. “What are these?” she asked the shopkeeper.

“They’re amulets,” he explained. “You can keep them in your car, at home …”

“And on your horse?” asked Isa.

“They’re especially good for horses,” said the shopkeeper, who clearly had a nose for business.

“I’ll take one,” said Isa, watching as he pushed a leather band through the eyelet.

“It’s a present for Felix. I’ve got just about enough money left to buy my little brother a comic at the airport. He’d be really upset if I didn’t get him anything.”

Tersia had discovered a box full of reddish stones – polished and engraved **carnelians**. “They’re so pretty,” she said admiringly.

“They’re from signet rings,” explained Hugo. “Some people make buttons out of them.”

“They’re much too nice for buttons,” said Tersia. “What do you think, Florentine? Maybe I should get one to put in a ring …”

Florentine was holding a net of thick silver chains in her hand.

---

matching – passend; mysterious – geheimnisvoll;
carnelian – Karneol

The shopkeeper told her in broken English that it was a **headdress** that used to belong to a nomad princess. It was very old, very unusual and, of course, extremely expensive.

Walter said: “If you like it, I’ll buy it for you.”

“Thanks,” said Florentine, “but I only accept presents for Christmas or birthdays.”

“What?” shrieked Tersia. “You’re such a dummy! Walter, buy it for me instead. Or get me this carnelian, hmm?”

Walter bought it.

Tersia flung her arms around him and kissed him **passionately**. Then she said in a loud whisper for everyone to hear: “I’ll make up it up to you with some ‘Sultan’s Delight’, OK?”

“How can you make such a fool of yourself?” said Nico in disgust. “Come on, Isa, let’s go.”

Jannik followed them. He was bright red in the face.

The last shop in the alley sold “antique” vases, oil lamps and mini sculptures. Bowls made of milky-white alabaster glowed in the half-light. Brass tins and tarnished mirrors gave off a dull shine. A smell of **joss sticks** and candles filled the air. A gust of wind blew down the alleyway, sending dust and little bits of rubbish flying. The cables jangled, and the light bulbs swung from side to side.

“It’s nearly dark!” said Isa in astonishment. “Is it really that late?”

“The storm’s coming in,” said Hugo. “Hurry up,

---

headdress – Kopfschmuck; passionately – leidenschaftlich; joss sticks – Räucherstäbchen

you guys, it's starting to rain. We'll have to find a bigger shop to shelter in … Do you want to look at some **rugs** and carpets? There's a carpet shop over here, and I know the owner."

The two men greeted each other with a ritual of back-slapping and a noisy exchange of questions: "How's life treating you? Are you well? How's business? And your wife and kids …"

The shopkeeper pulled up a couple of stools and a young boy came in with a tray made of beaten bronze. It was full of little cups of strong, dark coffee. Then his father got to work. He took one carpet after the next from the stack, unrolled them and started to explain their **patterns** and colours.

"This is boring," muttered Isa to Nico. "Who'd want to buy a carpet anyway? Florentine … huh, Florentine? Where's Florentine?"

"She was here just a second ago," said Hugo.

"She'll turn up soon," said Tersia **absent-mindedly**. She ran her hand over a rug made of delicate silk. "That would look good in my bedroom," she said to Walter. "What do you think of it?"

"But what about Florentine …" said Isa persistently. "I've got to find her. I'll be back in a second." She ran to the door, slipped out and was gone.

"Stop! Where are you going? Wait for me!" shouted Jannik. He tugged open the door … and then stopped in horror. That was no ordinary rain out there – it was the biggest, most incredible **downpour**. You wouldn't leave a dog outside in weather like that.

---

rug – Teppich; pattern – Muster;
absent-mindedly – geistesabwesend; downpour – Regenguss

"I'm not going out there," he said firmly.

"Those two cause nothing but trouble," said Walter grumpily.

Hugo glared at him. "You were the one who **insisted on** coming. If you'd stayed behind, you wouldn't have to worry about Isa and Florentine."

"What makes you think I'm worried about them? I'm cross with them, that's all. They're totally **irresponsible**. They're always getting some crazy idea or other into their heads. It's just not normal. They're both as chaotic as each other."

"Walter, darling," said Tersia, giving Hugo a sly wink, "you really shouldn't get yourself so worked up. With the rain coming down like this, we wouldn't be able to do anything anyway, so we may as well make the most of looking at these beautiful carpets … Look, here's some freshly brewed coffee for you. One sip of that and you'll soon feel more relaxed."

"It's far too late to drink coffee. I'll be up all night. I won't get a second's sleep," grumbled Walter.

"Nothing wrong with that," whispered Tersia, and kissed him on the ear.

The shopkeeper knew a business opportunity when he saw one. He fished out the silk rug that Tersia had said would look good in her bedroom and put it on top of the others. He displayed it first this way and then that in the dim light of the shop. He couldn't stop singing its praises.

"I can't stand it any longer," said Hugo suddenly. "You two go ahead and buy your rug. I'm going to look for Isa and Florentine. Are you coming, Nico?"

---

to insist on – bestehen auf; irresponsible – unverantwortlich

Nico was already standing in front of the window, yawning with **boredom** and looking out into the rain. "You bet!" he said in relief. "Which direction? Right or left?"

"Left, I reckon. The jewellery stall's our best bet."

They ran down the alleyway. Most of the shops were closed. The stall where Florentine had admired the princess's headdress was closed too.

Hugo and Nico banged frantically on the wooden door. They heard **dragging footsteps**, then somebody opened the door. They glanced inside the tiny little room, and realized immediately that the shopkeeper was the only person there.

"Sorry." Hugo stammered his apologies. "Bye!"

They were standing outside in the rain. It poured down on their heads and ran over their faces, making them look like a pair of **drowned** rats.

"Where next?" asked Nico.

"I'm thinking ... We're **soaked** now anyway, so there's no point in worrying about the rain. The shops are all closed though, and we can't go knocking on every door, asking for Florentine. But we can't just stand here doing nothing either. Maybe we should turn back?"

"I haven't got a better suggestion," said Nico.

A shadow flitted past them.

"Isa!" yelled Nico.

Suddenly the rain stopped, as if someone had turned off the taps.

"Did you find Florentine?" asked Hugo.

---

boredom – Langeweile; dragging footsteps – schlurfende Schritte; drowned – ertrunken; soaked – pitschnass

"No. I've got no idea where she is. But now the shops are opening again, maybe we can find her."

"Do you think we should go back to the carpet shop and collect the others first?" asked Nico. "Otherwise we might lose them too."

The shopkeeper was in the middle of **stacking** the coffee cups back on the tray. "So there you are," he called out. "Your friends left as soon as the rain stopped. They didn't buy anything – worse luck."

"I'm really sorry," said Hugo with genuine regret. "Which way did they go?"

The shopkeeper thought. "They went left … or was it right? No, it was definitely left … unless …"

"Don't worry," said Hugo, "the bazaar isn't that big. We're bound to find them."

Isa, Hugo and Nico set off. All the doors were opening again, people were laughing and chatting, and music was **blaring out** from countless different radios. Life was coming back into the alleyways, as if nothing had happened. The **cheeriness** was **contagious** – Isa would have liked to sit down, **leave** Florentine **to her own devices**. She wanted to just soak up the atmosphere, or better still, write it down. A little boy carrying a tray of coke bottles ran past her. A cat crossed the road ahead of him, making him stumble. The bottles toppled over and smashed to the ground. For a moment everyone fell silent. You could only hear the music – and the sound of Walter's voice.

---

to stack – aufstapeln; to blare out – dröhnen;
cheeriness – Fröhlichkeit; contagious – ansteckend;
to leave sb to their own devices – jmd. sich selbst überlassen

There was no mistaking it.

"... totally irresponsible," he was complaining.

"But darling! ..." That was Tersia's voice.

"What's it got to do with you anyway?" said a third voice.

"That's Florentine!" shouted Isa. "Hurray! We've found them all!"

Florentine was standing right at the end of the alleyway, in front of the antiques shop. She was clasping something to her chest. "I don't know why you're making such a scene," she hissed at Walter. "What I've been doing is none of your business. You've got no right to know!"

Hugo strode over to them. "What's going on?" he asked.

Tersia linked arms with Walter. "Just think, darling, if only you'd bought that lovely silk rug for my bedroom, you wouldn't be having this ridiculous argument now. Don't you agree, Jannik?"

"Argument? What argument?" thundered Walter. "I'm just annoyed with her for vanishing like that. I only asked her what she'd been up to. There's nothing wrong with that. Now, if I'd had my mobile with me –"

Isa came over to Florentine and took her hand.

"Why don't I buy you all a drink? I know we're all soaked," said Hugo, "but there's a place by the harbour where we can sit outside and look at the sea. That's the best **cure** for shattered nerves. OK, everyone?"

Nico took Isa's other hand and gave it a little

---

cure – Heilmittel

squeeze. She looked at him gratefully. "Do me a favour and stick around, will you?" she whispered.

It was a short walk to the pub near the **harbour**. They put two tables together, and Hugo ordered a bottle of wine, some water and a plate of hors-d'œuvres.

"Florentine, sweetie, why don't you show me what you bought?" asked Tersia, her **eyelashes fluttering** innocently.

"No, Tersia, sweetie, I don't want to," **spat** back Florentine.

"What a shame!" Tersia was playing with her newly acquired jewel. "I thought you didn't like secrets?"

"Too right." Florentine was trying not to **lose her temper**. "But that doesn't mean I'm totally naïve."

Hugo laid his hand on Florentine's arm, and started to tell a long and complicated story about some utterly hilarious incident that had happened at the beach club. No one was paying the slightest bit of attention and no one was remotely interested, but at least the story **served its purpose**. Everybody calmed down. After a while Florentine cleared her throat. "Hugo, I'd like to go back now, if you don't mind. Isa and I have got to pack. We're leaving first thing tomorrow morning."

No one spoke during the journey home. When they got to the club, Walter and Jannik quickly said their goodbyes and disappeared into the darkness.

---

harbour – Hafen; to flutter one's eyelashes – mit den Wimpern klimpern; to spit – fauchen; to lose one's temper – die Geduld verlieren; to serve a purpose – einem Zweck dienen

Florentine gave Hugo a quick hug. "I'm sorry," was all she said.

"I've got your address," said Hugo softly. "My parents live quite close by. I'll be visiting them in the autumn. Can I call you?"

"Of course. I'd like that. Are you coming now, Isa?"

"I'll see you on the plane tomorrow!" shouted Tersia cheerfully. "Good night. Enjoy your beauty sleep!"

"I'd like to know how that works," growled Nico. "I'll walk with you to your bungalow, OK?"

Isa said goodbye to him there. "And say 'bye' to the others for me too: Amelie, Senta – you know who I mean. And don't forget Jo either! When is it you're leaving?"

"Tomorrow afternoon. Well, I guess this is goodbye. **Take care** of yourself!"

"And you ..."

---

Take care [of yourself]! – Pass auf dich auf!

Florentine sat down on the bed and rested her bag on her lap. She carefully pulled out two packets, one very small one and the other a little bit larger. "I'm going to show you what I bought at the bazaar," she said to Isa. "You'll soon see why I had to disappear like that. They're both things that only you and I need to know about. Here you go – that's for you."

Isa **tore off** the packaging, eager to know what was inside. "Oh!" she exclaimed, "it's the ring that **matches** the earrings! It's so pretty! And it fits me perfectly. But why did you buy it for me? I should be the one buying you the presents – you paid for the holiday!"

"I just wanted to thank you," said Florentine earnestly. "You could have told me to stop chewing over my mouldy old relationship and throw it in the bin. But you didn't. You listened to everything I had to say, and that really helped me. I couldn't have had a better **travelling companion**. You're upbeat, uncomplicated, open and always ready for new adventures."

"If you don't stop now, I'll join the others in the disco," threatened Isa. "I really like the ring!" She

---

to tear off – etw. abreißen; to match sth – zu etw. passen; travelling companion – Reisebegleitung

held up her hand. “I wonder if there’s any matching nail varnish …”

“No idea. And now I’m going to show you what I bought for myself. It’s to draw a line under a long and sorry story.”

“A glass vase? But it’s so tiny. Daisies are about the only thing you can put in there.”

“It’s not for flowers, it’s for **tears,**” said Florentine softly. “**In ancient times** the rich **noblewomen** used to collect their tears in vases like this.”

“They must have had crying orgies,” said Isa. “I bet they cheated and used a bit of onion – no normal person could produce enough tears to fill a vase like that.” Isa laughed. “Do you think it’s real? I mean, is it a genuine antique?”

“I’d have to ask. But **it doesn’t** really **matter** anyway. For me the vase stands for the end of an era, thank goodness.”

They had almost finished packing when there was a knock on the door.

“Who can that be?” Florentine went to the door.

“Can we come in?” Walter was holding a bottle of wine in his hand, and Jannik was clutching some glasses.

“What do you want? We’ve only just said goodbye,” said Florentine.

“I want to renew my offer.”

“But I’m not interested.”

“Just hear me out.”

---

tears – Tränen; in ancient times – in der Antike;
noblewoman – Adlige; it doesn’t matter – das ist nicht wichtig

Some people were walking by. They stopped in front of the door and looked at them nosily.

"Come in then," said Florentine in irritation.

Walter **clumsily uncorked** the bottle. Jannik put the glasses on the coffee table and sat down on Isa's bed.

"About my offer," said Walter, "you see, working for my firm would give you the chance to take on some interesting responsibilities ..."

Florentine leant back against the wall and listened to him carefully.

When he'd finished speaking, she asked: "Is there an alternative?"

"You won't find a better offer," said Walter curtly.

Florentine nodded. "In that case I'll **turn** it **down** for the second and last time – totally, utterly, absolutely and definitively."

"But why?" he asked uncomprehendingly.

"I've got my own business to run, and I'm not about to give up my independence. But that's not the only factor. The other reason is that I don't believe in one-sided decisions. Here you are scheduling me into your plans and expecting everything to work on your terms. There's all this talk about team work and partnership, but what it comes down to is that I do the work and you profit from it. No, Walter, you'll have to find someone who's calculating enough to make your plans work for them."

Florentine went to the door and held it open.

"It's getting cold in here," said Isa.

---

clumsily – unbeholfen; to uncork – entkorken;
to turn sth down – etw. ablehnen

Jannik looked **downcast**.

"It's getting cold," repeated Florentine, "and I'd like to close the door."

When they were gone, Isa took a deep breath. "I didn't know you could be so tough."

Florentine pulled a face. "Nor did I."

She picked up the glasses and put them in front of the door. "You know, Isa, that's what really hurt me about Bert-Wolfram."

"How do you mean?"

Florentine thought for a moment. "Imagine you know that someone's keeping secrets from you. They're not telling you the whole story, so you start to ask questions. Then you dig a bit deeper and **put** them **under pressure**, but you still only ever hear part of the truth. You're getting more and more suspicious, but you're still supposed to act as if everything is normal. It's really mad."

Isa nodded. "Do you want me to write that down?"

"Yes, but there's more. No one ever tells you absolutely everything about themselves. You know that already, don't you, Isa? They'd be absolutely **unbearable** if they did. You'd think they were **self-important**, puffed-up **creeps**. We've all got the right to some privacy. But that right becomes a wrong as soon as we realize that our actions are hurtful. There's no hard and fast way of knowing when that is, so some people twist things to their own **advantage**. They talk

---

downcast – gedrückt;
to put sb under pressure – jmd. unter Druck setzen;
unbearable – unerträglich; self-important – selbstgefällig;
creep – Mistkerl; advantage – Vorteil

about letting 'sleeping dogs lie', even when the other person is **writhing** on the floor **in agony**. It's all a question of respecting yourself and empathizing with others."

Isa swallowed. "And a question of **dignity** too."

Florentine nodded. "The way I see it, people are at their most **vulnerable** when their dignity's been wounded."

"True. And how do you feel now? Have you managed to rescue your dignity? Is the worst behind you?"

Florentine looked at her vase. "I think so ... But there's more to it than that. In the olden days, women were financially dependent on men, so most of them didn't have any choice but to put up with everything and suffer in silence. These days it's different. Now women can take their lives into their own hands, and they expect to be treated as equals – not just at work but in their relationships too. That's why they don't accept men like Bert-Wolfram or Walter."

"Or Jannik," added Isa.

Florentine nodded. "But some men still don't get it. They're **trapped** in the past."

"That's a hell of a lot to write down." Isa stepped onto the patio and looked out to sea for a while before crawling into bed.

"Psst, Isa, wake up!" Florentine was shaking her.

"Hmm ... ?"

---

to writhe in agony – sich qualvoll winden;
dignity – Würde; vulnerable – verletzlich;
to be trapped – gefangen sein

Florentine put her hand over her mouth. “Psst! Come on, wake up!”

Isa was awake and listening.

“There’s someone on the patio, and we haven’t locked the door.”

Isa sat up. “So what? They won’t know that. It looks as if it’s locked,” she whispered. “What time is it?”

“Just gone four.”

“Already? It’ll be getting light soon.” Isa dragged herself out of bed.

What was that? Someone had **bumped into** one of the chairs on the patio. Isa rushed back into bed. She started **hiccoughing** in surprise.

“Maybe it’s – hick – a cat or something.”

“Or a dog. A great big dog. What if it comes in here?”

“And – hick – bites us! I’m going to lock the door. Hick!” Isa crawled out of bed again. She moved slowly and carefully towards the door, and **peeked out** from behind the curtain. “It’s pitch-black out there,” she whispered, “I can’t see a thing ... Oh yes, I can! There’s someone out there!” Isa froze.

“Hurry up and lock the door,” whispered Florentine. “Then at least we’ll be safe.”

Isa didn’t need telling again. She was already feeling for the **bolt**. It squeaked as she touched it.

“Hurry up!” pleaded Florentine.

Isa took her courage in both hands, grabbed the

---

to bump into sth – gegen etw. stoßen;
to hiccough – Schluckauf haben;
to peek out – hervorgucken; bolt – Riegel

**doorknob**, slammed the door shut and let the bolt snap into place.

"Couldn't you have done that more quietly!?"

"No!" Isa got back into bed and pulled up the covers.

They held hands, strained their ears and tried not to breathe. Someone was tapping on the window in soft, regular little knocks. The noise continued.

"God, that's got my adrenaline going!" Florentine giggled. "I'm not really laughing. I'm so scared I can't help it."

The knocking stopped. They heard the sound of **muffled** footsteps, then someone bumped into the chair again. It all went quiet.

"Are you sure the door's locked properly?" asked Florentine.

Isa nodded.

"Good. Then we can grab an hour's sleep before we have to get up."

Isa thought for a moment. She got out of bed. She **peered** out of the window, but couldn't see anything.

"Maybe I should go outside," she said.

"Are you crazy? What if someone's standing there with a knife? That's probably what he's waiting for – for you to go and look for him. Come on, get back into bed!"

Isa hesitated. "I'm going outside," she said firmly. She opened the door and stepped out onto the patio. She didn't have any shoes on, of course. She trod in something **squishy**, and couldn't help thinking of all

---

doorknob – Türgriff; muffled – gedämpft;
to peer – spähen; squishy – matschig

the revolting things it might be. She shrieked, slammed the door behind her, and leapt into bed. "Yuck! Someone's dumped something on the patio. I don't know what it is!" Her teeth were **chattering**.

"Walter's mobile," said Florentine suddenly. "If only we had Walter's mobile!"

"Y... you'd have to s... s... swim out and fetch it from the s... s... **seabed**!"

"Oh God, I'll be glad when this holiday is over. Which reminds me ..." Florentine felt her way to the wardrobe in the dark. "Here you go. I thought we'd had our last adventure, so I was going to leave the rum behind. Come on, take a sip, it will help to calm you down."

Isa drank and then coughed. "Remember to put the bottle in your hand-luggage. Who knows what'll happen next!" Isa pulled the duvet up under her chin. She gradually relaxed. After a while she fell back to sleep.

The alarm went off. For once in her life Isa was wide-awake immediately. She looked out onto the patio. "No," she said, not sure whether to be puzzled, excited or **concerned**. "I wonder who it's supposed to be for – you or me."

Florentine glanced over her shoulder. "It never rains but it pours."

There was a heart laid out on the patio. It was made up of the lilac-coloured flowers from the climbing plant on the **trellis**. It had been buffeted by the wind

---

to chatter – klappern; seabed – Meeresboden;
concerned – besorgt; trellis – Spalier

and had lost a few petals, but there was no doubt about it: it was clearly a heart. There was a piece of paper lying next to it, weighed down by a stone.

"For Isa – je t'aime. Love Jannik."

"That's really cute," said Isa. "But it's absolutely typical: only six words and he can't even **stick to** one language."

"Don't be so hard on him," said Florentine. "You should take a photo of it. It's not every day that you find a heart outside your window. I don't think anyone's ever done anything that sweet for me."

They were running so late that they had to **skip** breakfast. They struggled to get to reception on time.

"I bet we're not the last," panted Isa.

"No prizes for guessing who that will be!"

"Tersia."

But Tersia was waiting for them with her broad smile, blonde locks, tanned skin and tight-fitting leather trousers.

Florentine waved to her. "Did the 'Sultan's Delight' do the trick?"

Tersia faltered.

"Then double the **dosage**," Florentine advised her. She laughed. "And if that doesn't help, give up, and turn back to Bert-Wolfram. You can always send him to the doctor if he's worried about the **side-effects**."

Isa walked up to Jannik. "Thanks for the flowers," she said. "We woke up when you bumped into the chair. It gave us the shock of our lives!"

"I never do anything right." Jannik hung his head.

---

to stick to – sich auf etw. festlegen; to skip sth – etw. auslassen; dosage – Dosis; side-effect – Nebenwirkung

"Rubbish …"

"Come on, everyone, it's time to get going!" shouted Bridget.

Hugo, Jo and Hans came running. They kissed everyone goodbye and wished them a safe trip home.

# The Fracture

In the end, they needed all the luck they could get with their journey. Their flight home was the fitting finale to a week of holiday chaos. They got to the airport on time, but then the trouble started.

"I hope they serve us breakfast onboard," said Isa. "I've got a great big gaping hole in my belly."

"Don't worry," Florentine **reassured** her, "in less than twenty minutes we'll be enjoying a nice hot cup of coffee."

The island's little airport was already quite full. Babies were crying, young children were whining, **flustered** mums were waving brightly coloured dummies in the direction of the noise, and blank-looking dads were doing their best to act as if they had nothing to do with it.

**Urbane** businessman Walter drew on his extensive experience of flying to size up the situation. "Delays," he muttered, fishing his spare mobile out of his jacket pocket.

"How wonderful!" said Tersia. "That means we'll be able to spend soooo much more time together, Walter. Isn't that lovely?" Walter frowned and looked at her utterly **baffled**.

---

to reassure – jmd. beruhigen; flustered – aufgeregt; urbane – weltgewandt; baffled – ratlos

Isa grinned and winked at Jannik.

A group of young people in expensive outdoor kit booed and hissed at the news of the delay. Then they stopped messing about and proved they could handle anything. They squatted down on the floor, opened their backpacks, pooled their provisions and organized an **impromptu** picnic in the airport.

Tersia stared at them enviously. She looked first at Walter, who was **scowling**, and then back at the happy bunch, who were having a great time despite the early hour.

When Isa looked up again, Tersia was sitting in the middle of the backpacking **gourmets**.

"Do you fancy a coffee?" asked Florentine.

Isa nodded. "How about you, Jannik?"

"I bet you're even sleepier than the rest of us," said Florentine. "You must have been up all night making that heart. Come on, flower-boy, the coffee's on me."

It was a good investment. The "slight" delay lasted nearly three hours. Then the **announcement** finally came through, asking them to check in.

Isa and Florentine were allocated places at the back of the plane. And as if that wasn't bad enough, the window seat had already been taken. The man sitting in it was fat, short of breath, very sweaty and over two metres tall. The prospect of sitting next to him was so dire that Florentine asked to be re-seated.

"I'm sorry, but we're totally full. You'll have to make the best of it," said the stewardess.

---

impromptu – spontan; to scowl – mürrisch aussehen;
gourmet – Feinschmecker; announcement – Durchsage

"OK," said Isa, "I'll sit in the middle." She opened her rucksack and got out her notepad and pen.

Florentine had no choice but to take the aisle seat. "I don't like it when people keep walking past. You get a breeze every time," she said. "Not to mention the smell," she added quietly.

It wasn't long before the plane took off.

The man kept **mopping** his forehead and **shoving** his elbow half-way across Isa's seat.

"Hello! I'm still here, you know." Isa tried not to lose her patience.

"Is something the matter?" asked the heavy-breather.

"Your elbow is digging into me."

"Oh, sorry about that."

Once the plane reached **cruising altitude**, Isa's neighbour stopped looking so worried and started to entertain himself. He opened his newspaper. Isa's **misery** had only just begun.

The man was a champion in speed-reading. Either that or he only bought the paper for the headlines. He spread the newspaper out in front of him, letting his eyes race over the letters, before quickly turning the page.

Isa opened her notepad.

"A sporting week in the sun," she wrote. A piece of newspaper suddenly obscured her notepad. She could have read all about "A Night Full of Stars". The problem was, she wasn't interested.

She dug her elbow into her neighbour's flabby

---

to mop – abwischen; to shove – herüberschieben;
cruising altitude – Reiseflughöhe; misery – Elend

waist. He seemed to appreciate the contact and looked at her **affectionately**.

Isa dug a bit harder.

The man sighed and looked even happier.

That's no good, thought Isa, withdrawing her elbow.

The stewardess came around with the trays. Isa's neighbour made a grab for his breakfast, as if he were surviving on his very last grammes of fat. He asked for an extra bread roll and stretched his hand out **greedily**. The stewardess whipped away the bread basket, smiled at him brightly and used the tongs to deposit his extra ration on his tray.

He held out his cup, drank noisily and demanded a **refill**. Florentine laughed. "Do you want to **swap** places?" she sympathized.

Isa shook her head. "I'll survive."

The man grunted and concentrated on packing in the calories. Then he put his seat in the reclining position, so that he could sleep off his meal in comfort.

The passenger behind him protested noisily.

Adults, thought Isa. And I'm supposed **to look up to** people like that. She shook her head and read what she'd written: "A sporting week in the sun."

How on earth am I going to fit everything that's happened into one single article, she thought. It's impossible – there's far too much to write!

There was the water-skiing and snorkelling. That was all right – she could describe all that. But what

---

affectionately – liebevoll; greedily – gierig;
refill – Nachfüllen; to swap – tauschen;
to look up to – zu jmd. aufsehen

she'd **experienced** with the adults was a totally different ball game. She'd always thought that turbulent emotions were **strictly** for young people. In her mind, you reached a certain age, and things automatically calmed down.

Now she'd met people like Walter and Tersia, and she'd seen Florentine struggling with her past, and she felt like she'd been **duped**. She decided to talk to her parents about it. After all, they were the ones responsible for giving her such illusions. It felt like they'd stuck a tasty-looking, sweet-smelling, cream-covered piece of chocolate cake in front of her nose and told her: "Look! This is what people are like! This is life." But after she'd spent a week on holiday away from her family, it was as if someone had swapped the delicacy for a mouldy piece of biscuit.

She glanced over at Florentine. She was staring at a hole in the ceiling, deep in thought. "How are you feeling?" asked Isa.

Florentine jumped. "I was just thinking about a film by Woody Allen. One of his characters says something about the heart being a very **resilient** little muscle. You should write that down too."

Isa looked at her sceptically. "But is it true?"

"I think so ..."

"Hmm. I expect it **depends on** how well you've trained it – otherwise you'd end up with muscle ache." Isa remembered how she'd hardly been able to lift her arms up after water-skiing. "That would be awful."

---

to experience – erleben; strictly – ausschließlich;
to be duped – betrogen werden; resilient – hart im Nehmen;
to depend on – von etw. abhängen

"What?"

"Pulling your muscle."

Florentine put her hand on her heart in a theatrical gesture. "Hugo told me that even though it hurts when you pull a muscle, it's just your body's way of toughening it up after you've **strained** it."

Isa laughed. "Thank goodness the heart is a muscle and not a bone! A pulled muscle just needs a little rest, and then it's back in shape again. But imagine having to pin your broken heart back together again. You'd probably need a **splint** and a **plaster cast**! And even then there's no guarantee it would heal properly. I'm not very good at biology, but I do know there's always a little ridge where the bone's grown back together. The bone's always really fragile along the line of a fracture."

It wasn't long until the plane touched down. Isa rushed to collect her bags from the conveyor belt and to get through customs. She couldn't wait to see her family. Florentine was getting more and more hesitant the closer she got to the exit.

"We're back!" shouted Isa as soon as she spotted her family. She ran over to them, ruffled her younger brother's hair and let herself be hugged by her mum.

"Where's Dad?"

"He gave up his place in the car so that I could come too." Felix grinned and shoved an envelope into Isa's hand. "Welcome back! That's a message from Astra." He gave Isa a quick hug.

"Thank you! I've got some presents for you too. They're in my rucksack. I'll give them to you later."

---

to strain – zerren; splint – Schiene; plaster cast – Gipsverband

Isa peeked inside the envelope. "Wow! Hair from Astra's **mane** – that's cool! Thank you! How is she?"

"She missed you terribly," said Felix earnestly.

Isa sensed someone behind her. She turned around.

"We just wanted to say goodbye," said Walter.

Jannik was standing alongside him, staring **impassively**.

"Goodbye then – and take care!"

"Bye." Jannik was wearing his beloved sunglasses again. His eyes were totally hidden. He stuck his hands in his pockets. "Have fun telling them all about the holiday."

"Thanks."

"Goodbye, sweetie," Tersia gushed. "I'm sure we'll meet someday in town. Isn't that just wonderful? See you ..."

She swung around dramatically and waved at someone with both hands. "Hello honey! I'm home!"

"Bert-Wolfram ..." said Florentine. "I didn't expect to see him here."

Isa held Florentine's hand and gave it a little squeeze. She watched Tersia walk over towards Florentine's ex, her blonde ringlets swinging in time with her hips. She flung her arms around the stupid, disturbed, neurotic jerk, and **smothered** him with kisses.

He stood there stiffly, staring at Florentine.

Florentine took a deep breath. Then she pushed back her shoulders, let go of Isa's hand and walked energetically towards them. "If you need the **instruc-**

---

mane – Mähne; impassively – ausdruckslos;
to smother – ersticken;
instruction manual – Gebrauchsanweisung

**tion manual**, Tersia, I'd be happy to send it to you. I hope you enjoy yourselves. Goodbye."

Florentine swung her little black rucksack over her shoulder and headed for the door.

"Wow! Who was that?" asked Paul. "Do you know her? Was she in the same resort as you?"

"She's absolutely **awful**," said Isa. "If you were to get to know her, you'd see just how dreadful people can be."

"She's Bert-Wolfram's new girlfriend," said Florentine.

"Really? And she was at the beach club too? It's a small world," said Isa's mum in astonishment. "I can't wait to hear all your news. But let's get going – our parking ticket is bound to run out."

They ran to the car park and spotted a man in a dark-blue uniform checking the white tickets on the cars.

"It's going to be **tight** ..."

They were in luck. They beat the man to the car and quickly packed the luggage in the **boot**. Paul, Isa and Felix piled onto the backseat.

"Drive carefully," Isa warned her mum. "I hope you haven't been getting any more of those 'love letters' recently."

Isa's mum liked to drive fast. She was always forgetting to keep to the **speed limit**, so she often received "special letters" from the police. "Don't worry," she laughed. "Your dad did most of the driving in Tuscany."

---

awful – furchtbar; tight – knapp; boot – Kofferraum;
speed limit – Geschwindigkeitsbegrenzung

"How was your holiday?" Isa asked her younger brother.

"Cool, totally cool. We cooked for ourselves every single day. We had cocoa at breakfast, but the milk always **boiled over** and burnt, so we drank it cold instead. For lunch we cooked spaghetti and a separate pan of sauce. That meant we had to wash up two different pans, so in the end, we stirred the sauce into the water and then added the spaghetti. It looked like a great big pile of gunk! And for tea we had bread and spread."

"Spread? What do you mean?" asked Felix.

"Margarine, meat paste, cream cheese – you know, things you can spread on bread. It tasted really good, honest. We only **puked** – I mean, we only threw up once."

"And what else did you get up to?" asked Isa.

"We were always busy, you know, just doing things, ..." Paul made an expansive gesture. "There's too much to tell. I haven't got the time." He cleared his throat and changed the subject. "We thought, what with you being **delayed** and all that, you'd be sure to be hungry, so we got you something to eat. And we got something for ourselves as well – it's no fun eating on your own, is it?" said Paul. He reached back to the shelf behind him, and took down a bag. He handed out five cardboard boxes.

Isa opened the lid. "A burger," she said in delight. "A Big Mac. What do you say to that, Florentine?"

"Hmm ... half a burger-bun, a lettuce-leaf, a

---

to boil over – überkochen; to puke – kotzen;
delayed – verspätet

squashed bit of meat, cheese, a mushy slice of tomato, some watery gherkin, onion rings, mayonnaise, the top half of the bun and some sesame seeds – Isa, it's all there!"

"Forgotten what a Big Mac looks like or something?" Paul shook his head in disbelief.

"A big fat juicy burger," said Florentine. "The whole works."

"Don't you want yours?" Paul asked hopefully. "I can probably manage another one, if you really don't want it. Or maybe just half, if you can't eat it all."

"You wish! We're not into titbits, are we, Isa?"

"Women like us need the real thing," agreed Isa, taking a big bite of her burger.

Felix wiped a sesame seed from Isa's chin. "And so do men like me and Paul," he laughed.

Von Sissi Flegel bei Thienemann
bereits erschienen:

*Lieben verboten*
*Kanu, Küsse, Kanada*
*Liebe, Mails & Jadeperlen*
*Liebe, List & Andenzauber*
*Liebe, Sand & Seidenschleier*
*Coole Küsse, Meer & mehr*
*Schule, Ballett & erster Kuss*

Flegel, Sissi:
Forbidden to Love
Aus dem Deutschen von Sally-Ann Spencer
ISBN 3 522 17726 6

Reihengestaltung: Birgit Schössow
Einbandillustration: Birgit Schössow
Schrift: Stempel Garamond
Satz: KCS GmbH, Buchholz/Hamburg
Reproduktion: Medienfabrik, Möglingen
Druck und Bindung: Friedrich Pustet, Regensburg

6 5 4 3 2* 05 06 07 08

Thienemann im Internet: www.thienemann.de